Longman Structural Readers: Fiction
Stage 6

The Go-Between

L.P. Hartley

Longman

Longman Group Limited
London

*Associated companies, branches
and representatives throughout the world*

© 1953 by L. P. Hartley (Hamish Hamilton Ltd.)

*First published in this edition *1972
by arrangement with Hamish Hamilton Ltd.
New impression *1973*

ISBN 0 582 53783 5

*Printed in Hong Kong by
Dai Nippon Printing Co (H.K.) Ltd*

Acknowledgements

We are very grateful to MGM-EMI for permission to reproduce stills from the film 'The Go-Between', which was released through them in the United Kingdom.

We are also grateful to the Radio Times Hulton Picture Library for permission to reproduce the illustration on page 10.

Cover photographs from the film 'The Go-Between', released through MGM-EMI in the United Kingdom.

Contents

Prologue

I found the diary by chance. It was lying among some other things in an old red box. My mother had probably put them there many years before. They were the sort of things that every boy collects. I remembered the lock and the magnet immediately, but I could not remember the diary. They all looked old because, of course, they *were* old. I held a nail near the magnet in order to test its power. It still had enough power to attract the nail. It was enjoyable to recognize these things again. They were like children whom I had not seen for more than fifty years.

The diary puzzled me. It might have been a present that someone had given me. Perhaps it had come from abroad because the writing looked foreign. I noticed the gold on the edges of the pages. I felt sure that it had been one of my treasures. I am proud of my memory, but I could not remember anything about that diary. I looked at it for a long time but refused to touch it.

I picked up the lock. It was a special kind of lock, with three rows of letters. If someone moved the letters into the right position, the lock would open. I was the only person who knew the right position. I could arrange the letters properly even if my eyes were shut. The trick used to annoy my friends at school. They believed that I possessed some magic power, like the magnet. My skill gave me an advantage that was not altogether false. I had opened the lock so often that I needed only my sense of touch. But it was an effort that sometimes made me feel weak.

The letters now moved round between my fingers, and I shut my eyes. I tried to imagine that I was a little boy at school again. Other boys would be watching me. The letters moved slowly, and I felt each one. At last I found the right position. There was a faint sound, and the lock opened in my hand. At the same moment I remembered the secret of the diary.

It was a secret that frightened me. I remembered the disappointment and defeat that I had suffered. The message of that diary was quite clear. It told me that my character was weak; I pitied the weakness of my character. It told me also that I had not been strong enough to overcome my difficulties; I blamed myself because I had failed. When I found the diary I was sitting alone in a dusty room. It was cold and dark outside, but the curtains were not drawn. There were neither pictures nor flowers in the room. My mother's old things lay around me, and I was thinking about the past.

The diary contained an account of the events which had spoiled my life. If those events had never happened, I would have become a better man. I know that my life would have been different. I would probably have married and had children. My house would be a warm and bright place. My thoughts would be about the future, not the past.

I picked up the diary and opened it. On the first page I read:

Diary
for the Year
1900

The twelve signs of the zodiac appeared in a circle round the words, and I knew them well. They had been important to me when I was a boy. Each sign had suggested confidence, life and power. The smaller creatures were playing happily, and they represented young things and young people. The year 1900 was the first year of a new century. I was twelve years old in 1900, and I hoped for great things in the twentieth century. The big creatures of the zodiac represented the men who would rule the world. I intended to grow up as noble as they were.

The Virgin was the only lady in the circle. I did not know what she represented. Her long hair almost covered her, and she wore no clothes. I often thought about her, and gradually she became the chief figure in the group. I used to imagine that the zodiac was a kind of ladder. The fishes and the insects were standing on the bottom steps of the ladder. The animals stood above them, and the Virgin was at the top. She was their queen.

It was an exciting time, and I could hardly wait for the new century. 'Nineteen hundred, nineteen hundred,' I used to repeat to myself. I wondered whether I would be alive on January 1st 1900. I had doubts sometimes. Perhaps I would miss the experience of a new century. But I had a good excuse for these doubts. I had been ill the year before, and the idea of death was not strange to me. I tried to forget my fears and waited patiently for the new year.

I told my mother about some of my ambitions, and the diary was a present from her. She, too, hoped that 1900 would be a great year for me.

I was born on July 27th, and so the Lion was my particular sign of the zodiac. I admired the Lion and respected his strength. But he was not human. I wanted a human figure whom I could try to imitate. There were three in the zodiac, and I chose the Virgin. I hoped that she would help me in the twentieth century.

In January 1900 I had taken the diary back to school with me. And it had had one good result immediately. I knew the signs of the zodiac so well that my teachers were very pleased. But it had another, less fortunate, result. It was a beautiful little book, and 1900 was a very special year. So I decided that my diary should contain only important notes. They would be written in my best English.

I tried to remember the things that I had written. I turned the pages.

'Had tea today with Carter's parents. It was very nice.' 'Had a drive to Canterbury, very interesting.' 'Walked to Kingsgate Castle. Maudsley has a new knife.'

I turned the pages quickly. There were reports of games between my school and another school. We had played three times against Lambton House School, and at last we beat them. In my diary I had written: 'Lambton House VANQUISHED.'

Vanquished! I remembered that word very well. I suffered because I had written it. The diary was a private book, but I was very proud of it. I usually kept it in my desk, and I hoped to preserve its secrets. But I had to mention it to the other boys because, like the lock, it gave me an advantage. My reputation increased because I possessed a secret.

One day someone took the diary from my desk, and the secret was discovered. I was suddenly surrounded by a crowd of boys.

'Who said "vanquished"? Who said "vanquished"?' they shouted. They threw me to the ground, and a dozen boys pressed on top of me.

'Are you vanquished, Colston, are you vanquished?' someone shouted.

For a week after that they vanquished me every day. My body and my limbs felt sore, but I did not complain to the teachers. And I did not write to my mother about it. I knew that the punishment was my own fault. I should not have written the solemn word *vanquished*.

At the same time I was anxious to prove that I had not been vanquished. But I could not use force against a dozen other boys. I decided, therefore, to develop my magic power. The boys were afraid to keep a stolen article, and so they put the diary back in my desk. I decided to use it in order to punish them.

That evening I went to a small room where I was quite alone. I cut my finger with my knife and dipped my pen in the blood. I wrote two curses in the diary.

I am looking now at those faded signs and letters. I had invented the signs, and they did not mean anything at all. But I remembered the two names clearly. JENKINS and STRODE: they were the boys who attacked me most frequently. On the next page of the diary I had written:

CURSE THREE
AFTER CURSE THREE THE VICTIM DIES
Written by my hand and in my BLOOD
BY ORDER
THE AVENGER

I should have been ashamed of those curses because they were wrong, even wicked perhaps. But I was not ashamed of them then, and I am not ashamed of them now. Indeed, I envy the strength of character that I used to have. When I was young, I did not turn away from my enemies. I used to fight them in my own way. The victim of Jenkins and Strode always tried to be the avenger! I was determined that the other boys should respect me.

After I had written those curses, I put the diary in my cupboard. I left the door open so that the boys might see the little book. It was soon discovered by one of them. They attacked me again and beat me to the ground.

'Are you vanquished, Colston, are you vanquished?' Strode shouted. 'Who's the avenger now?'

Sitting across my shoulders, he pressed his fingers under my eyes.

It was a nasty experience.

That night, in bed, I cried. I had never been unpopular before, and I could not understand it. Maudsley was one of the boys in my room, and there were three others. They gave me no sympathy, and I asked for none.

The next morning somebody said to me, 'Have you heard the news?'

'What news?' I replied. I had hardly spoken to anybody for twelve hours.

'About Jenkins and Strode.'

'What's the news?' I asked.

'They climbed on to the roof last night. Jenkins slipped, and Strode tried to save him. He couldn't, and they both fell to the ground. They're in the hospital now.'

He looked at me curiously and then continued:

'I think they're both very ill. Jenkins's parents have just arrived and are already wearing black clothes. Strode's parents are due this afternoon. I thought you might be interested.'

I said nothing, and the boy went away whistling. I felt faint, glad and afraid at the same time. I was glad that Jenkins and Strode would not be able to attack me again. But I was afraid that they might die. Then everyone would blame me for their deaths. The school bell rang, and I walked towards the door. Two of the boys from my room came and shook hands with me. With respect in their faces, they congratulated me. I said a silent prayer of thanks to the Virgin and the Lion of the zodiac.

Jenkins and Strode had told all the boys about the curses, and my magic became famous immediately. Everyone wanted to know whether I was going to use the third curse. Many boys now thought that Jenkins and Strode deserved to die. But I decided to let them live, and my kindness was applauded. The result of the curses had secretly frightened me. So I wrote several new spells in order that my victims might get well again. I did not write them in my diary because they *might* fail. And I did not want my reputation to suffer. The school waited silently for several days, while everyone hoped for the worst kind of news. But the health of Jenkins and Strode improved a little, and they were taken home by their relations. I congratulated myself on the success of my spells.

'Are you vanquished, Colston, are you vanquished?' No, I was not. I had won a great victory, and I had won it in an unusual manner. But its most important quality was this: I had won it by myself, without any human help. After that, the boys of Southdown Hill

School always came to me when they wanted advice about magic or spells. I used to charge threepence for any help that I gave them. I also became famous as a master of language. *Vanquished* was my first long word, and it was followed by many others. The boys expected me to use them. It was then that I began to have ambitions: I would become a writer. Perhaps I would be the greatest writer of the greatest century, the twentieth.

In February, March and April 1900 I had written many notes in my diary, and most of these described my successes. There was not much in April because I was at home on holiday then. But May and the first half of June were full again, and then I reached the pages for July. On Monday July 9th I had written 'Brandham Hall'. There was a list of my fellow guests at the Hall. Then: 'Tuesday 10th 85 degrees'. Each day after that I had written the highest temperature and many other notes. At last I came to 'Thursday 26th 81 degrees'.

They were the last details I had written. I did not have to turn the other pages. I knew very well that they were all empty.

The main events of my life happened between July 9th and 26th 1900. They are my secret. They explain the kind of life that I have lived. For the past fifty years I have hidden them from the world, but I have never forgotten them. For fifty years all my time and strength have been given to my work, and in this way I have reduced the importance of my experience at Brandham Hall. I am sure now that this has been the best arrangement for me.

I know a lot more today than I knew in 1900. But my qualities of character were stronger then than they are now. If Brandham Hall had been the same kind of place as Southdown Hill School, I should have dealt with the problems in my own way. I understood my fellow pupils because they were a part of my life. But I did not understand Brandham Hall. The people there and their lives were different from those I knew. My fellow guests and our hosts seemed to possess all the mystery of the zodiac. They were the kind of people that I dreamed about. They represented my ambitions for the twentieth century, and they attracted me with the strength of a powerful magnet.

There, in my mother's dusty room, I imagined a conversation between two people. One of them was Colston when he was a boy, thirteen years old. The other was myself, Colston, at the age of sixty-four.

'Why have you become a miserable old man?' the boy asked. 'Your life is very uninteresting, isn't it? You've wasted your life in cheerless offices and libraries. You've studied other people's books, but you haven't written any books yourself. What has happened to those creatures of the zodiac whom you loved? Where are your favourites, the Virgin and the Lion?'

I answered immediately: 'It was your fault. You were like an insect that flies round a bright flame. You flew close to the flame, and you were burnt. That's why I am a dry, lifeless creature.'

The boy replied, 'But that was fifty years ago! Are you still suffering, after half a century? Don't you remember all your ambitions for the twentieth century? You thought it was going to be a wonderful time.'

I said, 'Has the twentieth century enjoyed greater success than I have? Is everything as wonderful as you expected? Are you pleased with the things that you see? I don't think so. You were vanquished, Colston, you were vanquished, and your wonderful century has been vanquished, too.'

'But you might have tried harder,' he answered. 'You needn't have accepted defeat without a struggle. I didn't run away from Jenkins and Strode, did I? I overcame them. They were my enemies, and I had to get rid of them. So I went to a quiet place and wrote three curses. Then Jenkins and Strode fell off the roof of the school and almost killed themselves. That was how I got rid of them. I was the avenger, and they were my victims. But have you shown any spirit like that? Have you prepared any curses?'

'That was your business,' I answered, 'and you didn't do it.'

'Oh, I did. I wrote a spell.'

'A spell was useless. Curses were needed then, not spells. You didn't curse Mrs Maudsley or her daughter or Ted Burgess or Trimingham. You didn't want to harm them because you liked them. You didn't believe that they had harmed you. You refused to think of them as your enemies. You thought they were as great as the creatures of your zodiac. Do you remember your advice to me? You said, "Don't think about those people at Brandham Hall. If you can't think about them in a kind way, don't think about them at all." I took your advice, and I've remembered it. There was very little kindness at Brandham Hall, but you didn't believe that. If you had cursed them properly, I would have become a better man.'

'Try now,' he said, 'try now. It isn't too late.'

The conversation ended, but it had had an effect on me. I *was* thinking about Brandham Hall. I remembered the scene, the people and the experience. It may not be too late, I thought. I will try to write the story. I began to feel excited.

It was very late. I picked up the lock again and turned it round in my hand. What was the secret of the letters that opened it? It was not a difficult question. I had not heard the word for many years, and I said it aloud. It was my own name, LEO.

Chapter 1

When I was at school, boys tried to forget their first names. I was Colston, not Leo Colston, and Maudsley was just called Maudsley. Later, perhaps, I shall remember his first name.

Maudsley and I were not special friends. With three other boys, he and I slept in the same room, and we knew one another well. He was pale, with fair hair and a round face. He was a year younger than I was. We often talked to each other and compared our private possessions. He was interested in my lock, and I admired his knife. He told me that he lived at Brandham Hall, in Norfolk. I told him that my home was Court Place at West Hatch, near Salisbury.

Maudsley seemed to have great respect for the name Court Place. He probably imagined that it was a large house in the country. His mother might have thought so, too, but they were both wrong. Court Place was quite an ordinary house in the main street of West Hatch. Part of the house was certainly very old and had once been a religious court. The name had remained. But it was not a big place, like Brandham Hall.

Although it was not a big house, the expenses were high. At that time my mother did not have a lot of money. My father had died when I was ten. He had been the manager of a bank in Salisbury, but that was only his profession. He was chiefly interested in books and gardening, and he had many strange ideas. He refused to let me go to school but taught me himself at home. We had very few friends. Neither my mother nor I liked these arrangements, and soon after his death we changed them. I went to Southdown Hill School.

I admired my father and respected his opinions; but I always felt nearer to my mother. He was not an ambitious man, and this lack of ambition used to annoy her. He bought many books and must have known their value. We did not share this pleasure until many years after he had died. We sold the books then and were quite astonished by the sale. It brought us more money than we had ever thought possible. But in the year 1900 we had only my mother's money and a small payment from the bank.

She was very different from my father. She liked meeting people and talking to them. She was fond of fashionable clothes and social occasions, but my father preferred to stay at home with his books. He sometimes took her to parties, and she enjoyed these very much.

Neither Maudsley nor I talked to each other about our families. In some ways he seemed already grown-up and was never in trouble with the other boys. He did not need the respect for which I had to fight. When I was losing a battle, he refused to give me any help. If I won some struggle, he used to congratulate me. He was always in agreement with public opinion, always on the winning side. I taught him how to write magic spells and did not make him pay for my advice. He admired me and my skills, and I enjoyed his respect.

I enjoyed, too, the weeks that followed the defeat of Jenkins and Strode. I had a great reputation for magic and a safe position among my fellow pupils. In April I went home for the holidays.

My mother did not really understand my success. She was pleased with the result of the examination but puzzled about my magic. I could not, of course, describe it to her in detail. I told her that a few of the boys had been unkind to me. Then I had written a kind of prayer in my diary. After that, the unkind boys had hurt themselves, and I felt glad about it.

'Was it right to feel glad, Leo?' she asked, anxiously. 'You should have felt sorry for them. Did they hurt themselves badly?'

'Rather badly,' I said. 'But they were my enemies, Mother.'

She refused to share my success, saying sadly: 'You're too young to have enemies, Leo. You must be kind to them when they come back to school. I'm sure they didn't intend to be unkind to you.'

Jenkins and Strode did not return to school until the autumn. When I met them again, they were very quiet. I was quiet, too, and we were certainly kind to one another.

When I went back to school early in May, my reputation was still strong. Many boys came to me for advice and urged me to write more spells. I agreed to write a spell that would gain a holiday for the school. I put all my magic power into this spell, and I soon received my reward. Two weeks later a fever struck the school. By the middle of June half the boys were sick, and the school had to shut its doors. The next day the headmaster told us that we would all have to go home. This was a wonderful success for me.

Both Maudsley and I escaped the illness. Our heavy cases were brought into our room, and we filled them with our clothes and other possessions. All that day we smelt the lovely smell of home. Next morning, two carriages arrived at the door of the school. There were usually three or four carriages, but the sick boys had already left the school. We cheered the headmaster and his family, and then we drove

We cheered the headmaster and drove off to the station.

off to the station.

In the train our high spirits continued, and there was joy in every face. Thoroughly happy, we sat along both sides of a private carriage. I took my diary out of my pocket and found the date. It was Friday June 15th. With a red pencil I drew a line under the date while the other boys watched me curiously. They probably wondered whether I was preparing some new spell. But I just filled the space with red lines.

I believed that I was partly responsible for the illness at school; and other boys thought so, too. I felt very confident of my power. If I *wanted* something to happen, it surely *would* happen. I was the master of my fate, and all natural laws were now my servants. My ambitions for the twentieth century looked clear and bright.

At home, my mother spoke to me about the fever at school.

'You'll probably be ill, too, Leo,' she said. 'You must tell me as soon as you don't feel well.'

I smiled. 'I won't get that fever, Mother,' I said. 'I'm sure I won't.' I did not tell her the truth: I would not get the fever because I did not *want* to get it.

'I hope you won't,' she said, 'but don't forget that you were very ill last year.'

I would never forget the year 1899 and its great unhappiness for me. In January my father had died after a short illness. In the summer I was seriously ill myself and had to stay in bed for seven weeks. July and August had been unusually hot months, too, but my own fever was even hotter. I can still remember my sore throat and the terrible heat of my bed. I was very glad when the summer ended.

I decided to arrange that the summer of 1900 would be cool. On July 1st I was pleased that the temperature reached only sixty-four degrees. There had been three hot days: June 10th, 11th and 12th; and I had marked them in my diary with a cross.

The invitation from Mrs Maudsley came on July 1st, and my mother showed me the letter. Mrs Maudsley was also a little worried by the thought of illness.

'If our boys are well on July 10th,' she wrote, 'they will probably escape the fever. And I would be very pleased if you allowed Leo to stay with us for a few weeks. Marcus often talks about him, and I would like to meet him. Marcus is my youngest child and will be glad to have a companion for the holidays. His brother and sister are several years older and have their own friends. If you agree, we promise to take great care of Leo. The air here is dry and very good for children. Neither my husband nor I were very well last winter, and we intend to stay here for the whole summer. I hope Leo will be able to stay with us until the end of July.'

Marcus. Yes, that was his first name. I remember it now.

I read the letter many times and could soon repeat it from memory. Someone who did not know me wanted to meet me. I believed that Mrs Maudsley was very interested in my character and my affairs. These were exciting thoughts. I did not guess that she might have written the same thing to any boy's mother.

At first my mother did not want me to go. She hesitated and made all kinds of excuses.

'Norfolk is a long way, Leo,' she said, 'and you've never stayed with another family before.'

'I've had to stay at school,' I argued.

'Yes, but you'll be away for two or three weeks, and you may not like it.'

'I'm sure I shall enjoy it, Mother,' I said.

'And you'll be there on your birthday. Have you forgotten that? We've always been together on your birthday.'

It was true that I *had* forgotten my birthday. It was not a very happy thought, and I did not answer.

'Will you promise to write to me if you're not happy?' she said.

I knew I should be happy. But I did not want to say that to my mother. I promised to write, but she was still not satisfied.

'You may get that fever,' she said brightly, 'or perhaps Marcus will. You won't be able to go then.'

I asked her a dozen times if she had written to Mrs Maudsley. Two or three days passed.

At last she said, 'Don't worry me, Leo. I have written, and you can go.'

Preparations were necessary. I had to decide about the things that I should need.

'I won't need summer clothes,' I said. 'I know it won't be hot.'

And I was right. The first days of July were quite cool, and my mother agreed with me. She believed that thick clothes were safer than thin clothes. But she had another reason: she could not afford new clothes for me. If I had wanted thin clothes for the summer, she would have bought them. But I was certain that the weather would be cool. And I did not want her to waste money.

'Try not to get hot,' she said. 'If you get hot, there's always a risk of illness. You needn't do anything *violent*, need you?'

We looked at each other in a puzzled way.

'No,' I said. 'I won't have to do anything violent.'

She liked to imagine Brandham Hall and the family there. 'Try to go to church if you can, Leo,' she said. 'I don't know what sort of people they are. Perhaps they don't go to church at all. If they do, they probably drive in a carriage.'

She enjoyed riding in a carriage, and she liked the thought of a large country house. She wished that she was going with me. But she did not say this.

Boys are often a little ashamed of their mothers, and I did not want her to come with me. I was afraid that she might wear the wrong kind of clothes. Perhaps she would say or do the wrong thing. It was always a problem when other boys, or their parents, were present.

On July 6th I began to feel afraid myself and did not want to go to Norfolk. But my mother now refused to change the arrangement.

'Write to Mrs Maudsley,' I begged, 'and tell her that I am ill.'

'I can't do that, Leo,' she said. 'It isn't true. You've been at home for three weeks. Mrs Maudsley would know that you weren't ill.'

I went to my room and wrote a spell. I wanted red spots on my body. But after two days no spots had appeared. On the last evening my mother and I sat together in silence. I think she wanted to advise me. But there were tears in my eyes, and she said nothing.

Chapter 2

I do not remember Brandham Hall very well. In my mind there are faint pictures of parts of the house, but the general view is not clear. My diary provides some of the facts.

I arrived on July 9th. That evening I wrote: 'Maudsley met me at the station, with a carriage, and we rode thirteen and three-quarter miles to Brandham Hall.'

I cannot remember that drive at all. I have even forgotten the look of the house when I first saw it through the trees. But I had studied a book about the district, and had copied some of the details into my diary.

'Brandham Hall is the home of the Winlove family. It is a big, rather ugly house on high ground, with gardens, a large park and a farm. The house contains pictures of the family and other scenes, all of which are the work of famous artists. The double staircase to the first floor is an interesting example of the builder's art. At present the house, gardens and park are rented by Mr W.H. Maudsley, of the City Bank, London.'

I thought the double staircase was the most beautiful part of the house. Its curve was more than half a complete circle. I compared it to many things: a magnet, a new moon, a horse's shoe. When I walked up or down those stairs, I used a different side each time.

Marcus and I slept together at the back of the house. There was a staircase there, too, and this was convenient for our room. I remember best those darker parts at the back of the house: the long, narrow passages, the sudden corners and the large number of doors. Our room had a broad window high in the wall. It was so high that we could see only the sky. Fifty years ago people did not worry about their children's rooms, and ours was not very nice.

Perhaps it was not easy to arrange places for all the guests. Many people came and went while I was staying at Brandham Hall. One evening, I remember, there were eighteen people at the table for dinner. I have never forgotten the brightness of the silver dishes and the small pink lights. The large figure of Mrs Maudsley seemed to command the table from one end, and the thin, straight figure of her husband was always at the other end.

Mr Maudsley was a slight little man and did not seem to be the master of the house. He had a long, thin neck and always wore high, stiff collars. I used to meet him suddenly on the stairs or in some passage, and he usually stopped. When this happened, our conversation was always the same. He said, 'Are you enjoying the holiday?' I answered, 'Yes, sir.' Then he always said, 'That's good.' He was often in a hurry, but I do not know where he was going.

His wife was clearly in charge of Brandham Hall, and in my memory she seems to have many faces. For fifty years she has been appearing regularly to me in my dreams. I have failed to keep her out of them. I actually saw her last on July 26th 1900. Her look on that occasion is the look that I remember most clearly. Her face then was so terrible that it was hardly a face at all. It was a big, round, pale shape, with eyes that were dark and fixed. Two or three wet black curls were hanging over the eyes. When I dream about Mrs Maudsley, I never see that terrible look. In my dreams her manner towards me is as kind as it was at the beginning of my visit. At that time I did not recognize the danger behind her influence. I suppose she was then between forty-five and fifty years old. Marcus had the same kind of round, pale face as his mother.

My first meal at Brandham was dinner on July 9th. I was a new guest and sat next to Mrs Maudsley.

She smiled at me and said, 'Marcus has told me that you know a lot about magic. Is it true?'

I replied modestly, 'Oh, not really. But at school, of course, everything is different.'

'Are you going to curse us here?' she asked.

'Oh, no.' I remember that I felt surprised and confused. I had never expected that Marcus would tell his mother about the curses. He ought to have kept the secret.

Mrs Maudsley never looked at anyone by chance but always with a clear intention. Her look usually meant that she did not agree; or that she was annoyed. She seemed to look most often at her daughter, Marian, but Marian hardly noticed the looks. Marian sat between two young men, and the three of them kept on talking during meals. I used to wonder what they were talking about.

Marcus had introduced me to everyone and told me something about each one. I wrote their names in my diary. The young people were generally single and only a few years older than I was. But those few years seemed wider than an ocean. Of course, we always greeted each other politely, and some of them spoke to me more than others. They were only a part of the scene at Brandham Hall and were never very important to me or to Marcus. But Marian *was* important.

Denys, Mr and Mrs Maudsley's elder son, was a tall young man with yellow hair. He had a high opinion of himself and also many other great opinions and plans. His mother did not have much patience either with Denys or with his ideas. She used to listen with attention and then quickly prove that his arguments were worthless. There was no real sympathy between Mrs Maudsley and her elder son, although he tried to be the man of the family. This was a position that his father should have held. But Mr Maudsley was quiet and did not seem to interfere with anyone.

I did not notice any lack of agreement between Mr and Mrs Maudsley. She made plans for the family and for the guests, but he made plans only for himself. The rest of us usually accepted her decisions without argument. If anyone had doubts, he would receive one of her looks. It made her intention quite clear and ended the discussion. It soon became clear to me that Mr Maudsley was a very rich man.

One day Marcus said to me, 'My sister is very beautiful.' This was a new fact that I had to learn. It seemed that he had just introduced me to her again. And when I saw her next, I looked at her closely.

Marian was very tall, and her eyes were very blue. They were bluer than any other eyes that I have ever seen. The sun was shining on her hair, making it bright. Her face was round, like her mother's, but the colour was pink instead of almost white. Her nose was small and curved. When I saw her, she might have been troubled. She was thinking about something, and her face had the look of some powerful bird. A moment later she looked up at me, and there was a great blue flash from her eyes.

After that I knew how to recognize beauty, and I could always recognize Marian among the other people at Brandham Hall.

In my diary I often referred to the horses which Mr Maudsley kept. They were important because they pulled the carriages. And the carriages were often used. I wrote down the names of five horses: Lady Jane, Princess, Uncas, Dry Toast and Nogo. The name Nogo amused me at the time, but I cannot remember him. He was probably a horse that refused to run.

My diary also reminds me of one thing which I had quite forgotten. It reminds me of the fact and of the exact scene.

'Wednesday July 11th. I saw the deadly nightshade—Atropa Belladonna.'

Marcus was not with me, and I was exploring some old huts behind the house. I had entered one which had no roof and suddenly saw the plant. It had already grown well and was about five feet tall. It was bright and strong and full of juice and seemed to be in perfect health.

'My sister is very beautiful.'

I could almost see the juice that was rising in its stem. In that old hut it had found the place that it liked best.

Atropa Belladonna, the deadly nightshade. I knew that every part of the plant was a strong poison. I had learned, too, that it was beautiful. I looked at its bright fruit and dark purple flowers. The flowers seemed to stretch out towards me. They would poison me, I thought then, even if I did not touch them. With a guilty conscience I crept away from the hut. I wondered whether I should tell Mrs Maudsley about my discovery.

Atropa
Belladonna

If I told her, she might be annoyed. And she would probably have the plant destroyed. I did not want anyone to destroy all that beauty. Besides, I wanted to look at it again, and so I did not tell her.

Chapter 3

At first I was in trouble with the weather.

It had been cool on Monday when I travelled. The next day it was hot, and the sky was cloudless. Marcus and I escaped from the house after lunch. We always hurried from the table as soon as Mrs Maudsley gave permission.

Marcus said, 'Let's go and see the thermometer. It's one that marks the highest and the lowest temperature of the day.'

I remember where the thermometer was. It hung on the wall of a mysterious building. The place stood in the shade of an old tree and often attracted me.

Marcus explained the instrument to me. He pointed to the small magnet which moved the markers up and down.

'This marker shows the highest temperature,' he said, 'and that one shows the lowest.'

I wanted to move the markers with the magnet, and Marcus must have guessed my thoughts.

'We mustn't touch it,' he said. 'It would make my father angry. He likes to take care of the thermometer himself.'

'Is he often angry?' I asked. I could not imagine Mr Maudsley being angry. I wanted to know the truth.

Marcus replied in a curious way. He said, 'No, but my mother would be.'

The temperature was nearly eighty-three degrees. The marker would probably move up to eighty-five by tea-time.

I was sweating slightly, and I remembered my mother's frequent remark. 'Try not to get hot,' she had said. How could I not get hot? I looked at Marcus. He was wearing a light suit. His shirt was not open, but it was loose at the neck. His trousers were loose round his knees. He had a pair of thin, grey stockings and light shoes. He was hardly dressed at all, I thought. But it was eighty-three degrees, and Marcus looked hot too.

I remember the details of our clothes. Marcus and I had our photograph taken, and the picture is in front of me now. It has faded, of course, because it is more than fifty years old.

I am wearing a stiff, white collar. My thick, woollen suit fits me tightly, from my neck to below my knees. The trousers are tied round my legs, below the knee. I have thick, black stockings and a pair of heavy boots.

My hand is on Marcus's shoulder, and I look fond of him. Indeed, I was fond of him, although we were never firm friends. Our characters were different, and we seldom enjoyed the same things. His round face is looking at the camera in a careless, satisfied way. My rather long face shows a trace of my trouble. In the photograph we are both wearing flat, round hats. His hat has a plain ribbon on it; mine has my school ribbon.

The heat was not a really serious nuisance. I still believed, partly at least, that I could influence the weather. That night I prepared a strong spell. I hoped that it would reduce the temperature. But I was disappointed. After lunch on Wednesday it was eighty-five degrees, and the little marker was still rising.

With an effort, I said to Marcus:

'Should I put on my games clothes?'

'No,' he replied, without hesitation. 'It's bad manners. No one should wear school clothes during the holidays. You oughtn't to wear that school ribbon round your hat. And, Leo, you mustn't wear your slippers at breakfast. It's a bad habit. I think bank clerks do it. You can put them on after tea if you like.'

I did not like his mentioning bank clerks. On Sundays my father had always worn his slippers at breakfast. But Marcus had not hurt me on purpose. I had never told him about my father's modest social position.

'There's another thing that you mustn't do, Leo. When you undress, you put your clothes neatly on a chair. You mustn't do that. You must leave them where they fall. The servants will pick them up.'

I believed every word that he said. I thought he was the leader of fashion and good manners. In the same way he respected my skill in magic.

At tea-time someone said to me, 'You look hot. Haven't you any lighter clothes?'

The words were spoken partly in fun. I wiped the sweat off my face and said, 'I'm not really hot. Marcus and I have been running.'

'Running?' said another voice. 'In this heat?' There was laughter in the voice, and I trembled a little. I imagined that I was at school again. And someone had shouted the word 'vanquished' at me.

Trouble started, although it was hidden by smiles and kind faces. At any time they used to say, 'Hullo, Leo. Are you still feeling hot? Why don't you take your coat off? You would be more comfortable without it.'

I hated these jokes. In those days, fifty years ago, everyone was particular about clothes. I took my coat off only when I went to bed. I knew that everyone was laughing at me; and I hated it.

That night I made a new spell. I felt so miserable that I could not sleep. My diary was under the pillow. I got it and managed to write the spell in the darkness. 'It will be stronger,' I thought, 'because it's in writing.'

I remember that spell succeeded. The next day the temperature did not reach seventy-seven, and I felt calmer and cooler.

I did not look cool, and at tea-time the jokes began again. At first they did not worry me because I knew the facts: the temperature was lower and I was cooler. But they continued, and soon I felt very miserable. I did not guess the intentions of the other people. They were trying to show kindness in order to make me talk.

I looked at myself in a mirror. For the first time I noticed my

clothes, and compared them with the others' clothes. I looked strange and unfashionable. I felt poor and common, and my face was red.

'I may look hot,' I said boldly, 'but I'm cool underneath.'

I thought it was a clever little speech. But everyone laughed loudly, and tears came to my eyes. I drank some tea quickly and began to sweat again. I wished that I had never looked in the mirror.

Suddenly I heard Mrs Maudsley's voice. It was like a current of cold air; and it was blowing towards me.

'Did you leave your summer clothes at home?'

'No . . . yes . . . Mother forgot to pack them,' I said.

This was a lie, and also an insult to my mother. She would have bought me lighter clothes if I had wanted them. I began to cry.

Mrs Maudsley said calmly, 'Why don't you write to her? Ask her to send them.'

I did not answer, but Marian spoke. I do not think she had ever mentioned the heat to me.

She now said, 'The post is too slow, Mother. I'll take him to Norwich tomorrow and buy some new clothes for him.' She said to me, 'You'd like that, wouldn't you?'

'Yes,' I whispered, 'but . . . '

'But what?'

'I haven't enough money. I have only fifteen shillings and eightpence.'

'We've got some,' Marian said.

'Oh, I can't take yours,' I objected. 'Mother won't like that.'

'Don't forget, Marian, that he has some things at home,' Mrs Maudsley said.

I felt very uncomfortable.

Marian said quickly, 'The new things can be a birthday present. His mother wouldn't mind that, I'm sure. When is your birthday, Leo?'

'It's . . . actually, it's on the twenty-seventh.'

'Of this month?'

'Yes. I was born under the sign of Leo. But Leo isn't my real name.'

'What is your real name?'

'It's Lionel. You won't tell anyone, will you?'

'Why not?'

'Because it's unusual.'

She tried to understand this mystery of a boy's mind. Then she said, 'That's splendid. You'll be here on your birthday. You can have something from each of us. Clothes are the nicest presents, aren't they? You're Leo the lion! If you were born under the sign of Leo, you should wear a lion skin.'

'That might be too hot,' I said in fun.

'Yes, of course,' she said. 'We'll go to Norwich tomorrow, Leo.'

'Perhaps you should wait until Monday,' her mother said. 'Hugh will be here then, and you can go together.'

'Who will be here?' Marian asked.

'Hugh. He's coming on Saturday. Didn't you know?'

'Is Hugh coming?' Mr Maudsley asked.

'Yes, he's staying until the end of the month,' Mrs Maudsley replied.

'Are you sure, Mother?' Denys asked. 'He told me that he was going to the races at Goodwood.'

'I had a letter from him yesterday,' Mrs Maudsley said.

'But he never misses Goodwood.'

'I think he intends to come here this year.'

'I don't want to argue, Mother,' Denys said. 'But Trimingham won't miss Goodwood Races.'

'He intends to miss them this year. Perhaps you should wait until Monday, Marian. Don't you agree?'

I had little patience with the conversation. I wondered who Hugh or Trimingham was. It would be a nuisance if he interfered with Marian's plans. I felt angry and jealous. If Trimingham came with us, the trip would be spoiled.

'Don't you agree, Marian?' Mrs Maudsley repeated. 'It will be better if you go on Monday.'

Marian had decided to go the next day. She answered immediately but not in agreement with her mother's suggestion. I imagined that two bare electric wires were rubbing against each other.

'Hugh won't enjoy it, Mother,' she said. 'He knows Norwich better than we do. He won't want to visit the shops in this heat. If we wait until Monday, Leo will have melted. Does anyone want to come with us?'

She looked boldly at everyone in the room. Her question was hardly an invitation, and no one wanted to come. I could not hide my delight.

'May we go, Mother?' Marian asked.

'Of course, unless your father wants the horses.'

Mr Maudsley shook his head.

'Go to Challow and Crawshay's,' said Denys suddenly. 'It's the best shop. Trimingham buys his ties there.'

'Does Leo need ties?' Mrs Maudsley asked.

'I'll pay for a tie if you promise to buy it at Challow's,' Denys said.
I began to feel hot again.

Marian decided to find out what things I needed. She had to
examine my clothes. I hated the thought of this enquiry, but I need
not have worried. When she came into our room with Marcus, she
was very kind. She looked at my things carefully.

'They have been mended beautifully,' she said. 'Our servants can't
mend clothes like this.'

I did not tell her that my mother had done the work; but perhaps
she guessed. She was able to guess things easily.

'You haven't any summer clothes at home, have you?' she said.
I agreed, and felt happy. I was glad to share the secret with her.
But I wondered how she knew.

Chapter 4

After the trip to Norwich everything was different. Buying clothes
usually annoyed me because I was not interested in them. I hardly
ever looked at myself in a mirror.

Marian and I went to several shops and looked at a lot of clothes.
I put on some of the things, and Marian liked them.

'That looks nice, Leo,' she said. 'It's just right for you.'

There were other things that she did not like. We did not buy them
because they did not look nice. In Marian's opinion it was most
important that clothes should look well. The things that my mother
bought for me had to be strong. They had to last for a long time. I
preferred Marian's idea, and it gave me a wonderful feeling.

We had lunch at a hotel, and it was a great event for me. My
father had always said that meals in hotels were too expensive.

After lunch we bought a few more things and took the parcels back
to the carriage. The front seat was covered with parcels.

'Would you like to change your clothes now?' Marian asked. 'Or
would you rather change at home?'

It was a question that I had to think about. It was hot in Norwich,
and I was wearing my thick suit. But I decided to postpone the
pleasure of changing mainly because I was too excited to feel the heat.
Everything seemed to depend on Marian's presence. She reminded
me of a bird with bright, flashing wings.

When we had bought all the things, she said: 'Leo, would you like
to amuse yourself for an hour? I have something to do. You can
visit the Cathedral.'

I agreed immediately. And when she left me, my delight continued.

A man near Marian had raised his hat. She was saying goodbye to him.

I knew of course that I would soon see her again. Inside the
Cathedral I looked up at the great arches of the roof. The building
seemed to express all my thoughts; it was high and wide and strong.
Later, when I stood outside, I looked up again. I tried to see the
exact place where the high tower seemed to meet the sky. All my
thoughts were as high as that great tower.

Marian and I had arranged to meet at four o'clock. When I reached
the carriage, the driver greeted me. I looked round for Marian and
saw her down the street. I noticed that a man near her raised his hat.
It seems clear to me now that she was saying goodbye to him. She
walked slowly towards me.

That day in Norwich my character seemed to change. I began to
feel like the other people at Brandham Hall. When I saw them all in
the evening, I was wearing my new clothes. The applause from
everyone was loud and long. I was told to stand on a chair and to
turn round. Everything was greatly admired.

'Did you get the tie at Challow's?' Denys asked. 'I won't pay for
it unless you did!'

Marian said, 'Yes.'

Actually, there was some other name on the tie; but I did not discover this until later. We had bought things at many shops!

'Doesn't he look cool?' someone said.

'As cool as the grass outside,' said another, 'and the same colour too.'

They discussed the colour of my new suit—green. I delighted in their remarks.

'Don't you *feel* different?' somebody asked me.

'Yes,' I exclaimed, 'I feel like another person.'

They laughed, and then the conversation changed. They began to talk about something which was not my new suit. I had enjoyed being the centre of attention. I got down from the chair.

Mrs Maudsley called me. 'Come here, Leo,' she said, 'and let me see you closely.'

I went to her anxiously. I felt like some insect that was trapped in a bright light. She rubbed the soft material of my suit between her fingers.

'I think it's very nice,' she said. 'I hope your mother will think so, too.' Then she turned away from me and spoke to her daughter.

'Oh, Marian, did you have time to buy those things I mentioned to you? We shall need them next week.'

'Yes, Mother, I bought them.'

'And did you buy anything for yourself?'

'Oh, no, Mother. I'll buy them later. There's plenty of time.'

'You mustn't wait too long,' said Mrs Maudsley, calmly. 'Did you meet anyone in Norwich?'

'Nobody at all. We were busy all the time, weren't we, Leo?'

'Yes, we were,' I answered. I was so eager to agree with her that I forgot my visit to the Cathedral.

I now began to enjoy the hot weather. I liked to feel the heat on my skin. The green suit was made of thin cloth, and it had an open neck. My trousers were also open at the knee. My new stockings were hardly thick enough to protect my legs from thorns. But I was especially proud of my new shoes, partly because they were just like Marcus's. All these things helped me to enjoy the heat of summer. As I have said, they also helped me to feel like the other people at Brandham Hall.

New clothes always seem to raise a person's spirits. I certainly could not hide the pleasure that I gained from mine. But I felt grateful, too, and very surprised. I was grateful for the goodness of my hosts because they had provided all these things. And I was astonished that the cost had seemed quite unimportant. In one morning Marian had probably spent on my clothes more than my mother spent in a year. Marcus's family must be richer than I had ever imagined. And there were other things that I could not understand. I did not know that rich people, like Mr Maudsley, did not need to go to work. I wondered why everyone seemed to be on holiday all the time. I tried to guess something about the families of the young men and women who came to stay at Brandham Hall. This last problem particularly interested me, and I explained it in my own way: I compared them with the ancient figures of the zodiac.

I now had a bathing suit and wanted to wear it. I could not swim unless somebody was holding me. Marian said that she would arrange that. But Mrs Maudsley refused to allow it.

'If you want to bathe, Leo,' she said, 'you must get your mother's permission. In her letter she said that you were delicate. I promised to take care of you. When the others bathe this afternoon, you had better watch them.'

I wrote to my mother immediately and then hurried away with the others. It was Saturday July 14th and the weather was a disappointment to me. The thermometer showed that the temperature was only seventy-six degrees. This was a secret that I shared with Marcus and his father. We laughed a little at the others because they were complaining of the heat. I took my bathing suit with me in order to feel in the right spirit. Marcus also had his, although he could not swim either.

When I was a boy, bathing was not a common exercise. Indeed, the experience was entirely new to me and the thought of it frightened me a little. I wondered what it was like in deep water.

We walked together down the path. There were Marian and Denys, another young man and a young woman, and Marcus and I. It was about six o'clock and still warm. We passed through a little gate and entered a group of trees. Among the trees it was dark and cool, almost cold. Later during the holiday, I often went that way through the trees, but I never again felt the same shock of coldness. We ran down a steep bank into a field, and it was hot again.

Marcus said, 'Trimingham is coming this evening.'

'Oh, is he?' I answered. I was not really interested, but I tried to remember the name. I wanted to add it to the list in my diary.

'Yes, but we shall be in bed when he comes.'

'Is he nice?' I asked.

'Yes, but very ugly. You mustn't look surprised by his face or it will annoy him. He doesn't like people feeling sorry for him. He was wounded in the war,[1] and his face hasn't got well again. The doctors

[1] The Boer War in South Africa, 1899-1902.

say it will never improve.'

'Bad luck,' I said.

'Yes, but you mustn't say so to him or to Marian.'

'Why not?'

'Mother won't like it.'

'Why not?' I said again.

'If I tell you, will you promise not to tell anyone?'

I promised.

'Mother wants Marian to marry him.'

I thought about this news in silence. I did not like it at all. I already felt jealous of Trimingham, and this news about his wound made it worse. Other people would have a high opinion of him because he had fought for his country. My father had hated war, and I agreed with him. Perhaps Trimingham deserved to be ugly. Mrs Maudsley should not want Marian to marry an ugly man. He was not even called Mr Trimingham. I felt very annoyed.

We came to the end of the field. A short distance in front there was a tall, black frame. It had upright posts and bars, and it frightened me a little. I wondered why we were walking towards it. Suddenly we saw a man's head and shoulders near the frame. His back was towards us, and he did not hear us. He climbed up the frame on to a shelf of wood. There he stood, stretching his arms and standing on his toes. For a moment he stood still, and then he dived off the shelf. I knew then that the river was near.

We all felt annoyed, and Denys must have felt angry.

'This place is private,' he said to us. 'That man shouldn't be here. What shall we do? Shall I order him to leave?'

'We'll have to let him dress first,' the other man said.

'He can dress in five minutes, and then he'll have to go,' Denys said.

'I'm going to change my clothes,' Marian said. 'I need more than five minutes for that.'

She went away with the young woman. There was a hut on the bank of the river, and the women changed there.

The water had been hidden until now, and we walked down to it. There was a pool that looked as blue as the sky. The only thing on its surface was the man's head. He saw us and began to swim towards us. We could soon see his face.

'Ah, that's Ted Burgess,' Denys said. 'He's the tenant of Black Farm. We shouldn't be rude to him. He rents the land on the other side of the river. Trimingham wouldn't like it if we were rude to him. I'll be very nice to him. He swims well, doesn't he?'

Denys seemed glad that he did not have to order the man to leave. But I was disappointed. I had hoped to hear some angry remarks. Ted Burgess did not look like a man who would be pleased to obey Denys's orders.

'I'll just say how do you do to him,' said Denys. 'He isn't one of our friends, of course; but he mustn't think that we're too proud to talk to him.'

Burgess climbed awkwardly out of the water, Denys helping him.

'Why didn't you get out comfortably?' Denys said. 'We've had some steps made on the other side of the frame.'

'I know,' replied the tenant of Black Farm. 'But I've always got out here.'

I remember his voice now. He spoke in the local manner, and this gave a kind of earnestness to his words. I thought he wanted to apologize to Denys.

'I didn't know that you would be here,' he said. 'The harvest has just started, and I was very hot. I thought I'd have a quick swim. But I won't stay long. I'll just have one more dive.'

'Oh, you needn't hurry,' Denys said. 'We were hot, too, at the Hall. Oh, did you know that Trimingham will be here tonight? He'll probably want to see you.'

'I suppose he will,' Burgess said. Then he climbed up to the shelf again and dived into the water.

Denys said, 'I don't think I made him feel uncomfortable.'

His friend agreed, and they went towards some bushes on the bank. Marcus and I went another way and soon found a place to change our clothes. We were completely hidden by the tall weeds that grew beside the river.

Marcus said, 'You needn't put on your bathing suit if you're not going to bathe. It would look strange.'

He always seemed to know the best thing, so I did not undress.

A few minutes later we all arrived at the steps beside the frame. I was disappointed when I saw the others' bathing suits. They seemed just like ordinary clothes. Marian's suit covered her more completely than her evening dresses. Denys and his friend pulled each other into the deep water. Marian, the other girl and Marcus stayed in the shallow water by the steps. At first they played, throwing up the water with their hands; and they were all laughing. Then the young women began to swim across the pool.

I did not like watching them, so I walked round to the other side of the frame. Denys and his friend were floating on their backs. While I was admiring them, Ted Burgess climbed out of the water.

Ted Burgess did not look like a man who would be pleased to obey Denys.

Marian's suit covered her more completely than her evening dresses.

I moved back among the weeds where he could not see me; and I watched him.

His body looked so powerful that it almost frightened me. It was something that I had never seen before. He walked away from the bank and lay down on the warm ground in the sun. What did it feel like, I wondered, to be as strong as he was? He did not need to play games or to do exercises. His body was complete and perfect and existed for its own strength and beauty. The lower part of his arms and his neck were burnt brown by the sun. The rest of his body was so white that it might have belonged to another person.

Suddenly a cry came from the river: 'Oh, my hair! my hair! I've lost the ribbon, and it's all wet! It'll never dry now. What shall I do? I'm coming out!'

Ted Burgess sprang up. He did not dry himself. He pulled his shirt and trousers on, over his wet bathing suit, and put on his socks and boots. In half a minute he was dressed. Then he walked quickly away through the weeds. He cursed at something as he went.

A moment later Marian came out of the water. She was holding her long hair in front of her, like the Virgin of the zodiac. She saw me immediately and seemed happy and angry at the same time.

'Oh, Leo,' she said, 'you look so pleased with yourself that I'd like to throw you in the river!'

Her words alarmed me, and perhaps I looked afraid. She then said, 'I don't mean that really. But you're very *dry* and I'm very *wet*. I'm sure my hair will never dry.' She looked round and added, 'Has that man gone?'

'Yes,' I said. I was always glad to answer any question she asked me. 'He went in a hurry. His name is Ted Burgess, and he's the tenant of Black Farm. Do you know him?'

'I may have met him,' Marian said. 'I don't remember. But I'm glad that you're still here.'

I did not quite know why she was glad; but it sounded like praise. She went to the hut. Soon the others came out of the river. Marcus began to tell me how much he had enjoyed the bathe. I envied his wet bathing suit. My dry one seemed to tell me that I had failed. We had to wait a long time for the ladies. But at last Marian came out of the hut, still holding her hair in front of her.

'Oh, I shall never get it dry,' she cried. 'And the water is running over my dress.'

I was surprised to hear Marian talk like that. Her hair was wet, and she was behaving like a child. Women were very curious, I thought. Suddenly I had an idea, and it filled me with joy.

'Here's my bathing suit,' I said. 'It's *quite* dry. You can put it round your neck so that it hangs down your back. Then you can spread your hair on it, and your hair will soon dry. Your dress won't get wet either.'

That seemed to be the longest speech that I had ever made. I felt quite breathless. I held the suit up so that Marian might consider the suggestion.

'It might be a good idea.' she said. 'Has anyone a pin?'

Somebody gave her a pin. The other girl hung the bathing suit round Marian's neck, and everyone congratulated me on my cleverness.

'And now you must spread my hair on it,' she said to me. 'And please don't pull it. Oh, Leo!'

I knew that I had not hurt her. I had hardly touched her hair. Then I saw that she was smiling. I started again, arranging it gently over my bathing suit. It was a duty that I loved; partly, perhaps, because I loved Marian.

I walked back with her through the shadows. Once or twice she asked me how her hair was. In order to answer her I had to feel it. She pretended then that I had pulled it. She was strangely excited, and I was, too. In some way I thought that we were both excited for the same reason. But I could not have explained this idea. I believed that I had done a wonderful service to Marian. At the Hall she took off the bathing suit and gave it back to me. It was damp with the dampness from which I had saved her. She let me touch her hair. It was dry with the dryness that I had gained for it. I had never felt happier in my life.

Chapter 5

Breakfast at Brandham Hall started with prayers, and these were read by Mr Maudsley. The servants always attended this ceremony. Marcus told me that there were twelve servants. I counted them every morning, but there were never more than ten present. Mrs Maudsley was always there. Denys and Marian came sometimes. Marcus and I seldom failed to arrive early. About half the other guests used to attend. The chairs were arranged round the walls. It was a good time to observe the guests and the servants, especially the servants.

Marcus knew them well, of course, and he knew some of their secrets. If one of them was in trouble, he always knew the reason for it. Prayers would be more interesting if one of the servants came in with red eyes. I tried to guess the cause of her crying.

It was Sunday July 15th; my first Sunday morning at Brandham Hall. Marcus did not come down to breakfast with me. He did not feel well and wanted to stay in bed. He looked hot and his eyes were bright.

'Don't worry about me,' he said. 'One of the servants will soon come up. Give my greetings to Trimingham.'

I decided to tell Mrs Maudsley about Marcus. I was anxious about his health and rather liked telling bad news. I waited until the bell rang at nine o'clock, and then went down the double staircase. I easily remembered the side that had to be used.

What was Trimingham like, I wondered. He was not called *Mr* Trimingham, but Mrs Maudsley still wanted her daughter to marry him. Perhaps Marian did not want to marry him. There would certainly be some trouble if Marian's wishes were hindered. I felt quite sure of that. Trimingham was a nuisance, and perhaps I should put a spell on him. I began to think of the right words for it.

I reached my favourite chair. The other guests were coming in, and one of them sat down beside me. I immediately knew who it was. In spite of Marcus's advice, I could not hide my shock.

His face looked terrible. Between one eye and the corner of his mouth there was the great curve of a wound. It pulled the eye down and the mouth up. I did not think that he could shut that eye at all. His mouth, too, was probably always partly open. His whole face was the wrong shape. The side with the wound was much shorter than the other.

I have tried to remember my exact thoughts when I first saw Trimingham. First I decided that I could not possibly like him. And when I had decided that, I immediately liked him better. I was certainly not afraid of him, but his social position was still not clear to me. It was not so high that it deserved the word *Mr*, but it was probably higher than Ted Burgess's position. Because of his wound, I thought, everyone treated him very politely. But perhaps he was a poor relation of Mr or Mrs Maudsley, and they were kind to him for that reason. I decided, then, to be kind to him myself.

At breakfast he sat beside Marian, and so I could not mention the greetings from Marcus. Several guests had arrived on Saturday night, and the table was full. Mrs Maudsley was very busy. During the meal she looked often and directly at Trimingham. She did not look at me until we were all leaving the table. Then she said: 'Oh, isn't Marcus here?' She had not noticed that he was absent.

She went to his room immediately. A few minutes later I followed her. She was not with Marcus when I arrived.

'What's the matter?' I said.

'You'd better not stay here,' he replied. 'My head is aching, and I have some spots. It may be the same fever that the boys had in school. Mother didn't say so, but I know.'

'That's bad luck,' I said. 'We left school weeks ago.'

'The doctor is coming. He'll know what it is. It will be fun if you get it, too. Perhaps we'll all get it. Then we shan't be able to have the cricket match or the ball or anything. Oh, I shall laugh!'

'Are we going to have a cricket match?' I asked.

'Yes, we have one every year.'

'And a ball?' I asked. I was rather frightened of dancing.

'Yes. That's for Marian and Trimingham, and all the neighbours. It will be on Saturday 28th. Mother has sent all the invitations, but the house will be like a hospital by then!'

We both laughed; Marcus said, 'You'd better go. You're breathing all my germs.'

'Yes, I am probably. I want to get my prayer book.'

'Are you going to church?' he asked.

'Yes, I think so.'

'You needn't if you don't want to go.'

'Perhaps I ought to go. Shall I rush across the room for my prayer book?'

'Yes, but don't breathe.'

Standing by the door, I filled my lungs with air. Then I rushed to the table, picked up my prayer book and hurried back to the door.

'Good,' said Marcus. 'I didn't think you would manage to do it.'

I struggled to get my breath. Marcus reminded me that I should need some money for church.

'Mother will probably ask you about it,' he said.

I waved goodbye to him and ran down the double staircase.

Several people were waiting at the front door. I admired the beauty of the women's prayer books; the men seemed to have hidden theirs. I was wearing my thick suit. Marcus had said that that was right. I could put on my green suit after lunch.

Mrs Maudsley called me to her and put some pennies, into my hand 'That's for church,' she said.

Mr Maudsley took his watch out of his pocket and looked closely at it.

'Shall we wait for Trimingham?' he said.

'We can wait another minute or two,' his wife replied.

My mother was wrong: we did not drive to church in a carriage. It was only half a mile away, just beyond the cricket field. We walked in small groups. Marian probably noticed that I was alone; and she walked with me. I told her about Marcus.

'Oh, he'll soon be well,' she said. 'The heat worries some people.'

'Is your hair quite dry now?' I asked, anxiously.

She laughed and said, 'Yes. I was glad to have your bathing suit.'

I felt proud of my idea, but conversation with her was not easy. I asked another question about her hair, and it made her laugh again.

'Haven't you any sisters?' she said.

That annoyed me, because I had told her about my family. I reminded her of one of our conversations in Norwich.

'Of course you told me,' she said. 'I remember it perfectly now. I have many things to think about. I'm sorry that I forgot about your family.'

I had never heard Marian apologize to anyone before. I had a strange feeling of sweetness and power, but I could not say anything to her. I looked at her face, at her large hat and at her light blue skirt. Her skirt made a track through the dust as she walked. Suddenly I noticed that Trimingham was following us. He was walking quite quickly and would soon catch up with us. I did not want him to do that; but I did not know how to avoid it.

'Trimingham is coming,' I said. It sounded like bad news.

'Oh, is he?' she said. She turned her head but did not call to him. When he caught up with us, he smiled. He walked past us to the people in front, and I felt very glad.

Chapter 6

In church I sat with the family and their guests. Our seats were a little higher than the other seats. When I sat down, a man offered me a prayer book. I proudly showed that I had my own. On one wall of the church there were brass plates with the names of dead people on them. I noticed that the name Trimingham appeared on each one. 'In memory of Hugh Winlove, Sixth Viscount Trimingham,' I read. 'Born 1783, Died 1856.' I studied the names with care. Most of the Viscounts had been called Hugh. There were seven altogether, but there should have been nine. The fifth Viscount was missing, and there was no plate for the ninth Viscount either. The last name was Hugh, Eighth Viscount Trimingham, born 1843, died 1894.

I felt annoyed with the list because it was not complete. The fifth Viscount was not mentioned at all. But the eighth Viscount had died in 1894, and so there must be another.

Suddenly the idea came to me that the ninth Viscount might still be alive. If that was true, it would change my opinion of the family. The names on the wall were a part of history. The old Viscounts had fought in battles and had won great honour. A few had been ministers in the government. But they were all as dead as the names in my history books. If there really was a ninth Viscount, he would probably be alive. He was not yet a part of history. He was a part of today, just as I was. The church, the village and Brandham Hall belonged to him. I wondered where he was.

Thinking about this, I decided to give part of the honour to Mr Maudsley. He should enjoy it because he rented Brandham Hall. And if he enjoyed it, then I should enjoy it, too; because I was one of his guests.

I did not like being in church for a long time. I was fond of singing and had learnt one or two religious songs. They were a great pleasure to me, but prayers were different. I had no patience with some of the prayers. The priest's words often referred to the wickedness of men. It was not true, I thought. I did not believe people were really wicked.

In my opinion, people behaved in natural ways. Sometimes their actions caused pain or unhappiness. I thought of Jenkins and Strode.

35

Were they wicked boys? No. They were boys like myself. Their deeds had annoyed me, and I had to do something in order to protect myself. I did not ask God to have mercy on them. I fought them in my own way, and I won. The victory was mine, not God's.

I felt sure that God agreed with me. He admired me, I thought, because I had not begged for his help. Life had its own struggles, and these tested any man. They proved his courage, and courage was a good thing.

When I was young, I had great respect for goodness. In my opinion, it was not the opposite of wickedness. It was something strong and bright, like the sun, and did not change. All the Viscounts whose names I had read seemed to possess goodness. The Maudsley family seemed to have it too, perhaps, I thought, because they paid a rent for it. I believed that they were all part of a different race from ordinary people.

I looked at my watch. It was ten minutes to one. We stood up and went out of the church. Outside, I was alone again. Marian went

Trimingham was talking to the priest at the door.

ahead with some other people, but I was not last in the procession. Trimingham was talking to the priest at the door. The respect that everyone showed to Trimingham still puzzled me. I was thinking about this when he caught up with me.

He said very politely, 'We haven't been introduced yet. My name is Trimingham.'

At that time my experience of social customs was slight. I did not know that I ought to mention my own name. Indeed, I thought then that he was rather stupid. Did he imagine that I did not know his name?

'How do you do, Trimingham?' I replied, stiffly.

'You may call me Hugh if you like,' he said.

'But your name is Trimingham, isn't it?' I said. 'You told me it was.' But I wanted to show him that I was polite, too. And I added quickly: 'Mr Trimingham, I mean.'

'You were right the first time,' he said.

I looked at his terrible face. I wondered whether he was trying to make a joke.

'Aren't all men called Mister?' I asked.

'No, not all. Doctors aren't, are they?'

'But that's different. "Doctor" is a title.'

'I have a title, too,' he said.

And then, very slowly, I understood the truth. It was something that I had never imagined.

'Are you *Viscount* Trimingham?' I asked.

'Yes.'

'Are you the *ninth* Viscount Trimingham?'

'I am,' he said.

The news was a shock to me, and for a few moments I could not say anything. I felt annoyed then because no one had told me. I ought to have guessed, of course. It had been plain from the start, and it explained the politeness and the respect.

'Oughtn't I to call you my lord?' I asked.

'Oh, no,' he said, 'not in ordinary conversation. On some occasions perhaps you should, but Trimingham or Hugh is quite good enough.'

I was astonished now that he spoke in an ordinary way. I had to change my opinion of him very quickly. The old Trimingham faded from my life. The ninth Viscount almost filled it. And I believed that he was nine times as distinguished as the first. I had never met a lord before. I had never even expected to meet one. I did not care how ugly he was. He was a lord, and that was the most important thing.

'You haven't told me your name,' he said.

'It's Colston,' I said, with some difficulty.

'Mr Colston?' he asked, gently.

'My first name is Leo.'

'Then I shall call you Leo if you agree.'

'Please do,' I said.

'Does Marian call you Leo? I noticed you were talking to her this morning.'

'Oh, yes, she does,' I replied eagerly. 'And I call her Marian, too. She told me to do that. Don't you think she's a wonderful girl?'

'Yes, I do,' he said.

'She's the nicest girl I've ever met,' I said. 'I'd do anything for her.'

'What would you do?'

I suspected that the question was a trap. Perhaps he thought that I was boasting. I could not really do anything important for her.

I said, 'If a big dog attacked her, I would frighten it away. I could carry things for her, too, and be her messenger.'

'That would be a great help,' Lord Trimingham said, 'and it would be kind, too. Will you take a message to her now?'

'Of course. What shall I say?'

'Tell her that I've got her prayer book. She left it in church.'

I hurried away. Marian was walking with a man whom I had not met. I did not interrupt their conversation, but a moment later they stopped talking.

I then said to Marian: 'Hugh asked me to give you a message. He said he had your prayer book. You left it in church.'

'That was careless, wasn't it?' she said. 'I seem to forget everything. Please thank him for me.'

I ran back to Lord Trimingham and repeated Marian's remarks.

'Is that all she said?' he asked. He seemed disappointed. Perhaps he wanted her to come and claim the prayer book immediately.

At the Hall a small carriage with black and yellow wheels was standing outside the front door.

'Do you know whose carriage that is?' Lord Trimingham asked.

'No.'

'It's Dr Franklin's. Doctors always come at lunch-time, don't they? It's one of their customs.'

'How did you know it was Dr Franklin's carriage?' I asked boldly.

'Oh, I know everyone in this part of Norfolk,' he said.

'Of course, it all belongs to you really, doesn't it?' I asked. Then I said something that I had been thinking about. 'You are a guest in your own house!'

He smiled. 'Yes, and I'm very pleased about it,' he said.

After lunch Mrs Maudsley said to me, 'Marcus isn't very well. The doctor said that he must stay in bed for a few days. We don't think it's a fever. But you'd better not see him until he's well again. The servants are moving your things into another room. It's a room with a green door. Shall I show it to you?'

'Oh, no, thank you,' I said. 'I know the room with a green door.'

I hurried away. I wondered whether I would have to share the room with another guest. It would be strange if I had to share a bed, too. I paused at the green door and then knocked quietly. No one replied, and so I went in. My fears melted away. It was a small room, with a very narrow bed, just big enough for one person. My things were all there. I checked them quickly: hair brushes, clothes, cases. They were all in different places, and they looked different. The room made me feel different, too. I imagined that I had a new character.

I remembered Marcus's suggestion. I put on my green suit and prepared to go out. There was a spirit of adventure about all my actions. I crept down the staircase, and went out of the house. I am certain that no one saw me.

Chapter 7

The temperature was eighty-four degrees, and I wanted it to rise higher.

There had been no rain at all, and I was enjoying the heat. It seemed to make my ambitions stronger. I was not now satisfied with a boy's simple experiences. I wanted larger experiences and more of them. Perhaps I had always had these desires, and they might have been connected with my love for the zodiac. Several events had given me a taste of power: my diary, the attacks of Jenkins and Strode, the curses and the spells. Now I was close to the wealth of the Maudsleys and the greatness of the Triminghams. These new experiences must have encouraged me to dream of power, and soon my dreams began to confuse me. I began to feel that I was a part of the zodiac. It was probably the heat that made me think in this way.

Marcus was in bed, and I had to amuse myself. In the afternoons we had usually played behind the house, but I now decided to go further. I walked along the path that led to the bathing place.

I was wondering whether Ted Burgess, the farmer, would be there. But no one was swimming, and the silence of the place frightened me. I climbed the platform from which the farmer had dived. I looked down into the clear water. It was like a mirror. I crossed a low bridge to the other side of the river and came to a field of corn. The corn had just been cut, and some of it was lying on the ground. There was a gate in the opposite corner of the field, and I walked towards that.

From the gate a path led between fields to a low hill. It turned left then and ended at a small farm house. It was a place that was full of adventure and experience for me. Perhaps I should meet a fierce dog, or there might be a straw stack. I loved sliding down straw stacks. There was no one near the farm.

I opened the gate and went in. There, in front of me, was a straw stack with a convenient ladder beside it. It was an old stack, half of which had been cut away. But I could slide down the rest of it.

I climbed the ladder to the top of the stack and then slid down. The rush through the air delighted me. It was wonderfully cool. I imagined that I was flying. But at the bottom my knee hit something hard. It was a log of wood that was buried in the straw on the ground. I watched the blood as it flowed from a long cut just below my knee. The fate of Jenkins and Strode flashed through my mind. I wondered whether I had broken any bones.

I had no time to think about the accident. The farmer came out of the house, carrying a bucket of water in each hand. It was Ted Burgess. I remembered him immediately, but he did not remember me.

'Who are you?' he cried; 'and what are you doing here?' He was very angry. 'I think I'll beat you hard.'

His voice frightened me. I remembered how strong he was.

'But I know you!' I cried. 'We—we've met before!'

'Met?' he said. 'Where?'

'At the bathing place,' I said. 'You were bathing by yourself, and I came with the others.'

'Ah!' he said. His voice and manner changed completely. 'You must be from the Hall.'

'Yes.' The pain in my knee was worse now, and I touched the wound. Ted Burgess was looking at me.

'I'd better wrap something round that,' he said. 'Come to the cottage. Can you walk?'

He helped me to get up, and I went with him.

'You're lucky,' he said. 'It's Sunday today. If it was any other day, I wouldn't be here at this time. I heard your cries.'

'Did I cry?' The news was a shock to me.

'You did,' he said. 'But some boys would have cried a lot louder.'

I enjoyed his praise. I thought that perhaps I ought to praise him,

'Some boys would have cried a lot louder.'

too.

'I saw you diving,' I said. 'You did it very well.'

He seemed pleased, and then said: 'I'm sorry I was angry. I have a quick temper. I didn't know that you were from the Hall.'

I thought that his change of manner was quite natural. It was right and proper, too. Had I not changed my opinion of Lord Trimingham? He told me that he was a Viscount. And I changed my opinion of him immediately. Ted Burgess and I had the same ideas about respect for other people.

We entered the house. I thought it was a very poor place.

'This is where I usually live,' he said. 'I'm not a rich farmer who pays men to work for him. I do most of the work myself. Sit down, and I'll get something for your knee.'

He washed the cut and then poured some special liquid on to it. It had stopped bleeding.

'You were lucky,' he said. 'You might have torn your trousers or your stockings. You might have spoilt that nice green suit.'

I agreed with him. I had been very lucky. 'Miss Marian gave it to me,' I said. 'Miss Marian Maudsley, at the Hall.'

'Oh, did she?' he said. 'I don't know those people very well. I'll wrap this round the cut.'

'This' was an old handkerchief.

'But won't you need it?' I asked.

'Oh, I've got plenty of them.'

I thought that my question had annoyed him. He pulled the handkerchief hard. 'Is it too tight to bend your knee?' he asked.

I stood up and walked about. My knee was beginning to feel better. I was already planning the story that I should tell at Brandham Hall. But I owed something to the farmer. I would not have offered him money even if I had had any. But perhaps I could give him a present. I looked round the bare kitchen. I wondered whether he needed anything.

Then I said: 'Thank you very much, Mr Burgess. You've helped me a lot. Is there anything that I can do for you?'

I quite expected that he would say 'No'. But I was wrong. He looked at me closely and said:

'Perhaps there is. Will you take a message for me?'

'Of course,' I said, but I felt disappointed. I remembered that Lord Trimingham's message to Marian had not been a great success. 'What is it, and who shall I give it to?'

He was still looking at me. Then he said, 'How old are you?'

'I shall be thirteen on the twenty-seventh of this month,' I replied.

'I thought you were older than that,' he said. 'I wonder if I can trust you.'

His doubt gave me a shock, but I was not really annoyed. I thought that he was going to tell me a secret.

'Of course you can trust me,' I said proudly. 'My mother has just had a report from my school. It said that anyone could trust me.'

'Yes, but can I trust you?' he said, slowly. 'My message will be a secret one.'

I thought he was very stupid. He clearly did not know anything about a schoolboy's honour. 'Do you want me to swear that I'll tell no one?' I asked.

'You can do anything you like,' he answered. 'But if you tell anybody—'. He did not finish the sentence, and I understood the threat. It seemed to fill the room with a sense of power.

'Isn't there another boy at the Hall?' he said.

'Yes, my friend Marcus,' I replied. 'But he's ill.'

'Oh, he's ill,' he repeated. 'And so you are alone, are you?'

'Yes, but he'll soon be well again,' I said.

'It's a big house, isn't it? How many rooms are there?'

'I don't know.'

'And there are a lot of people there, I suppose,' he said. 'Are you ever alone with anybody?'

'Sometimes,' I said. 'But they're older than I am. They play games together and talk a lot. I talked to Viscount Trimingham this morning. And once I went to Norwich with Marian. She's Marcus's sister and a wonderful girl.'

'Oh, you went to Norwich with her, did you?' the farmer said. 'Are you one of her special friends?'

'She's different from the others,' I said. 'She talks to me quite often. She talked to me this morning while we were going to church.'

'Oh, did she?' the farmer said. 'Are you alone with her sometimes?' He spoke with great earnestness. I thought that he was trying to imagine the scene.

I said, 'Sometimes we sit together, after dinner perhaps.'

'You sit together,' he repeated. 'Are you near enough to—?'

'Near enough?' I said. 'Of course, her dress spreads out—'

'Yes, yes. These dresses spread out a long way. But are you near enough to give her something?'

'Give her something? Oh, yes, I could give her something,' I said.

'Could you give her a letter? A secret letter?'

It was such a simple request that I almost laughed. 'Oh, yes,' I said. 'I can do that.'

'I'll write it now,' he said. 'You'll wait, won't you?'

'Oh course. But how can you write to her when you don't know her?'

'Who said I didn't know her?' he asked.

'You did. You said you didn't know the people at the Hall. And Marian told me that she didn't know you. She said that she may have met you; but she didn't remember you.'

The farmer thought about this problem for a moment. Then he said, 'She does know me. I don't visit the Hall, but we do some business together.'

'Is it a secret?' I asked, eagerly.

'It's more than a secret,' he said.

I suddenly felt weak, and Ted Burgess noticed this.

'Sit down,' he said. 'I'll soon write this letter.'

He brought a bottle of ink, a pen and a sheet of paper. But he was not used to writing. His fingers seemed too big to hold the pen.

'Shall I just tell her the message?' I said.

'You wouldn't understand it,' he replied.

At last he finished writing the letter. He put it in an envelope and stuck it down. I stretched out my hand, but he did not give me the letter.

'Don't give it to her unless you are alone with her,' he said.

'You can be sure of that,' I said.

I thought, then, that he would really give it to me. But he held it tightly in his hand. He was like a lion guarding something with its paw.

'Can I trust you?' he said.

'Of course you can,' I answered. His doubts annoyed me now.

'If any other person reads it, there will be plenty of trouble. There will be trouble for her and for me and perhaps for you, too.'

'I shall defend it until I die,' I said.

He smiled, opened his hand and pushed the letter towards me.

'But you haven't written the address!' I exclaimed.

'No,' he said, confidently, 'and I haven't written my name on it either.'

'Will she be glad to get it?' I asked.

'I think so,' he said.

'And must she answer it?' I wanted to be sure about the details.

'She may answer it,' he said. 'But don't ask questions. Why do you want to know everything?'

I did not answer him but looked at my watch. 'It's late,' I said. 'I must go now.'

'How does your knee feel?' he asked.

'There's no pain. And it isn't bleeding now.'

'It may bleed when you walk,' he said.

I hoped it would bleed. I wanted to arrive at the Hall with blood on the handkerchief. I put the letter in my trousers' pocket.

'May I come and slide down your straw stack again?' I asked.

'Of course. And I'll move that log of wood.'

He walked with me to the gate, and we waved goodbye to each other.

At Brandham Hall I received a lot of sympathy. My knee became the subject of conversation. I explained that Ted Burgess had been very kind.

'Ah, he's the tenant of Black Farm,' Mr Maudsley said. 'I've heard something about him. He's a strong young fellow and rides a horse well.'

'Yes. I want to see him,' Lord Trimingham said. 'He'll probably play in the cricket match on Saturday, and I'll talk to him then.'

I wondered if Ted Burgess had done something wrong; and I

looked at Marian. But she was not listening to the conversation. The letter was still in my pocket. Marian suddenly stood up and said:

'I'd better wash your knee, Leo. That handkerchief isn't very clean.'

I was glad to follow her up the stairs. She made me sit on the side of the bath and took off my shoe and stocking.

'Now put your knee under the tap,' she said. 'You've got a nasty cut.'

She washed the wound and dried my leg. Then she wrapped a clean cloth round it. Ted Burgess's handkerchief was lying on the side of the bath. It was stained with blood.

'Is that his handkerchief?' she asked.

'Yes. He said he didn't want it. Shall I throw it away? I know where the rubbish heap is.' It was not far from the hut where I had seen the deadly nightshade.

'Perhaps I'll wash it,' she said. 'It's quite a good handkerchief.'

Then I remembered the letter and took it out of my pocket.

'He asked me to give you this,' I said.

She pulled it out of my hand. She had no pockets. And she did not know where she could put the letter.

'These dresses are a nuisance,' she said. 'But wait a moment.'

Taking the letter and the handkerchief, she left the room. A moment later she came back and said: 'Now I must wrap up your knee.'

'But you've already done it!' I said.

'Of course I have! What am I thinking about? I must put on your stocking.'

'Oh, I can do that myself,' I said. 'It's no trouble.'

But she wanted to do it, and I did not object.

'Are you going to answer the letter?' I asked.

She shook her head. 'You mustn't tell anyone about the letter.' She was looking away from me. 'Don't tell anyone, not even Marcus.'

Her fear and Ted Burgess's fear puzzled me very much. They did not seem to know that it was a lot easier to keep silent than to speak.

'You needn't worry,' I said. 'I won't tell anyone. I can't tell Marcus, can I? I'm not allowed to see him.'

'Of course,' she said. 'I seem to forget everything. But if anyone finds out about the letter, we shall all be in terrible trouble.'

Chapter 8

Before Lord Trimingham arrived, everyone at Brandham Hall had behaved in a very ordinary way. It was true that Mrs Maudsley had directed most of our affairs. But in spite of that, we had usually been able to please ourselves. Lord Trimingham's presence seemed to change everyone's manner. We spoke with care and behaved less freely than before. It was like the time of examinations at school: an anxious time for everybody.

Mrs Maudsley planned something different every day. There were walks in the country. We had lunches or tea-parties in the park. We visited interesting places, travelling in the carriages. Mrs Maudsley made her suggestions after breakfast. They always sounded like commands to the rest of us. But to Lord Trimingham they were questions which were carried to him by one of her direct looks.

'That's a splendid idea,' he might say; or, 'I hoped we might do that.' He always agreed with her plans for the day.

I remember one of our trips very well. We were all sitting beside a stream. The servants were unpacking the baskets of food and spreading the rugs on the grass. I enjoyed the meal and the cool drink from a bottle; but I hated all the conversation. I sat near Marian, but she did not look at me. She was interested only in Lord Trimingham sitting beside her, but I could not hear their

'*You know who Mercury was, don't you?*'

46

conversation.

After a time Lord Trimingham looked up and said, 'Ah, there's Mercury!'

'Why do you call him Mercury?' Marian asked.

'Because he carries messages,' Lord Trimingham said. Turning to me, he said, 'You know who Mercury was, don't you?'

'I think he was one of the ancient gods,' I said.

'That's right. He was the messenger of the gods, too. He was their go-between.'

The messenger of the gods! I felt very proud. I was a traveller through heaven, visiting one god after another. It was like a wonderful dream that soon became a real dream. Lying on the bank of that stream, I went to sleep. When I woke up, I did not open my eyes immediately. The others might laugh at me because I had gone to sleep. Marian was talking to her mother.

'He doesn't enjoy these trips with us, Mother,' she said. 'He likes wandering about alone.'

'Oh, do you think so?' Mrs Maudsley asked. 'He loves being with you, Marian.'

'And I love him,' Marian said. 'But he's only a child, Mother. We're not very interesting companions for him.'

'I'll have to ask him about that,' Mrs Maudsley said. 'When he comes with us, there are thirteen people; and thirteen is an awkward number. Marcus's illness is very unfortunate.'

'Yes. We may have to postpone the ball,' Marian said. 'And the cricket match has been arranged, too.'

'We won't postpone the ball,' said Mrs Maudsley firmly. 'We can't disappoint all the people we've invited. You wouldn't like that, Marian, would you?'

I did not hear Marian's reply, but I noticed again the lack of agreement between her and her mother. They never argued fiercely in the presence of guests, but there were often clear differences of opinion between them. I opened my eyes then and stood up. Lord Trimingham was looking at me.

'Ah,' he said, 'Mercury is awake again. He has had a little rest.'

I smiled at him. There was something in his character that did not change. I always felt safe with him. His opinion of me would remain the same even if I made some mistake. His conversation with the others often sounded quite foolish, but it never annoyed me. I remembered the facts: he was Viscount Trimingham; he had fought in a war and had been badly wounded. He never complained. Our little problems were not very important to him. He laughed at them, and he laughed at our jokes. No matter what happened, he was always calm.

When we went home that evening, I sat beside the driver of the carriage. The conversation was easy. We understood each other perfectly. I asked all the questions, and he answered them. If he did not know the answer, he would say so. We dealt only with facts, and I was very fond of facts. When I talked to the others at Brandham Hall, I could never discover the facts of the conversation. With them perhaps, it was the conversation of the gods! I was their messenger. And a messenger need not understand the messages that he carries.

Marian's suggestion that I should not go with them on these trips had annoyed me at first. But I remembered her words: 'I love him.' They were like a sweet taste in my mouth. Of course I enjoyed the drives through Norfolk; but Marian was right. There were things that I did not enjoy. I preferred the old huts, the bathing place and the straw stack. I even preferred the heap of rubbish. They were all places that interested me. I wanted to visit them all again. I remembered then that beautiful plant, the deadly nightshade: Atropa Belladonna. And I wanted to see it again.

'Do you know Ted Burgess?' I asked the driver.

'Oh, yes,' he said, 'we all know him.'

'Do you like him?'

'We're all neighbours,' he said. 'Mr Burgess likes a bit of fun.'

I noticed that the driver said *Mr* Burgess. But I did not know why he referred to 'fun'. Ted Burgess did not seem to have much fun.

At last we came to the exciting part of the drive. There were two steep hills. We had to drive down the first and up the other. At first the weight of the carriage pushed the horses forward, and the driver had to struggle with them. I imagined all the accidents that could happen. But we reached the bottom safely, and both carriages stopped. All the men got out in order to make the work easier for the horses. I asked the driver if I could get down, too.

'Why?' he said. 'The horses won't worry about your weight.'

I was not very pleased to hear that. But he helped me to get down, and I walked up the hill with the men.

Lord Trimingham was hot. He touched his face with a silk handkerchief. He was wearing a white suit and a white straw hat.

'You look very cool, Mercury,' he said to me. 'This must be the hottest day of the summer.'

At the top of the hill, the men got into the carriages again, and the journey continued. I remembered what Lord Trimingham had said about the heat. I hoped that it *was* the hottest day of the summer.

When we reached Brandham Hall, I intended to read the thermometer; but this was impossible. Tea was ready, and there was a letter from my mother. I looked at the address with pride: Leo Colston, Brandham Hall, near Norwich. It was a splendid address.

I read the letter in my room, and it did not really interest me. At school I always enjoyed my mother's letters, but this one had a different effect on me. Her news of home seemed unimportant now. I did not feel that I was a part of her life. My proper place was here, at Brandham Hall, I thought. Here I was a small god who carried messages for the other gods. Her remarks about the heat annoyed me a little. She ought to know that I was enjoying it.

I tried to answer her letter, but the result was not a great success. I could not explain all the thoughts that were in my mind. They seemed to be on a higher level than she would understand. I wrote about Viscount Trimingham, Marian and Marcus:

Viscount Trimingham called me Mercury because I carry messages for people. Marcus's sister, Marian, is still very nice to me, and I like her more than the others. I am sorry that she is going to get married. But she will then be a lady Viscount, and that will be wonderful.

I did not know why these thoughts made *me* feel important. And I was not sure that my mother would understand them.

I told her, too, that Marcus was not very well. But I did not say anything about a fever. I wrote about our visits to various places. I mentioned the cricket match, the party on my birthday and the ball. She had said that I might bathe; and I thanked her for this. I promised not to bathe unless someone was with me. It was not a very good letter, but I did not finish it until six o'clock.

I hurried away, then, to look at the thermometer. I expected something unusual, and I was not disappointed. The temperature was eighty-five degrees, but the little marker had been pushed up to ninety-four. Ninety-four! That was doubtless the highest temperature that had ever been reached in England. I wondered whether it would reach a hundred tomorrow. It was my ambition that it should. The sun could surely produce another six degrees, I thought.

All my thoughts seemed to lead to greater heights. I felt very excited. And I imagined that all my companions were excited, too. We were climbing a ladder of great experiences: Norwich, the cricket match, my party and the ball. The high temperatures were only a part of the excitement. I was not quite sure about the events that would follow the ball. But they were connected with Marian and Lord Trimingham. Perhaps they would marry. There was pleasure in that thought, too. I would have to sacrifice the part of me that found its happiness in her.

I heard a voice behind me. 'Are you enjoying yourself?'

Mr Maudsley had come to examine the thermometer. I answered him politely.

'It's been hot today,' he remarked.

'Has it ever been hotter?' I asked eagerly.

'I don't think so,' he said, 'but I'm not sure. Do you like hot weather?'

I said that I did. He picked up the magnet in order to move the markers. I did not want to watch him, so I said something quickly and hurried away.

Crossing a part of the garden, I heard another voice. It was Lord Trimingham's.

'Come here!' he called. 'We want you!'

I did not want to talk to anyone. I preferred to be alone with my own exciting thoughts. But he came to meet me.

'You're always wandering about,' he said. 'Can you find Marian for me? We'd like her to play a game with us. We've looked for her but can't find her. I'm sure you know where to find her. You must bring her here alive or dead!'

I ran off. I did not know where she was. But I knew that I should find her. I went round to the back of the house because that was the most interesting part to me. I ran down the path towards the old huts. I remembered that the deadly nightshade lived in one of them. Then I saw Marian. She was walking rather quickly up the path. When she saw me, she did not smile.

'What are you doing here?' she said.

We had stopped beside each other. There was more colour than usual in her face, and she was breathing quickly. I felt guilty for some reason, but I answered immediately. I thought she would be pleased.

'Hugh asked me to tell you—' I began, and then stopped.

'Yes? What did he ask you to tell me?'

'He asked me to find you—' I said.

I waited for her smile, but it did not come. She looked up and down the path and seemed annoyed about something.

'But what did he say? Have you forgotten?' she asked.

It was the first time her voice had sounded unkind to me. My face probably showed that I was hurt. And her manner changed then.

'I know it isn't easy to remember everything,' she said. 'But what does Hugh want?'

'He wants you to play a game with them.'

'What time is it?' she asked.

'Nearly seven o'clock.'

'We don't have dinner until half past eight, do we? There's plenty of time. I'll go.'

We were friends again, and we walked back together.

'He told me to bring you dead or alive,' I said.

'Oh, did he? And which do you think I am?'

I thought that was a good joke. Then she said:

'We're going to have lunch with some neighbours tomorrow. They're old people, as old as the hills. Mother thinks you might not be interested. Do you mind staying here?'

'Of course not,' I replied. I remembered that this was Marian's idea, not her mother's. But it was not very important.

'What will you do to amuse yourself?' she asked.

'I'm not sure yet. I might do several things.'

'Tell me one of them.'

'Perhaps I'll walk somewhere.'

'Where?'

I had an idea then that she was guiding the conversation. I wondered what she wanted me to say.

'I might slide down a straw stack. It's great fun.'

'Whose straw stack?'

'Perhaps Farmer Burgess's.'

'Oh, his?' She sounded very surprised. 'Leo, if you go to his farm, will you do something for me?'

'Of course. What is it?' But I knew before she told me.

'Give him a letter.'

'I hoped you'd say that!' I exclaimed.

'Why? Is it because you like him?'

'Yes. But I like Hugh more, of course.'

'Ah, that's because he's a Viscount, perhaps.'

'Yes, that's one reason,' I said, without any false shame. I had real respect for Hugh's rank. 'But he's gentle, too. He doesn't give orders to people. I thought a Viscount would be proud.'

She considered my remarks.

'And Mr Burgess,' I continued, 'is only a farmer.' I remembered his angry remarks to me at the straw stack. He did not know then that I was a guest at the Hall. 'He's a rather rough man, I think,' I added.

'Is he?' she said. 'I don't know him very well. We sometimes write notes to each other, on business of course. You said you'd like to take them.'

'Oh, yes, I would,' I said, eagerly.

'Is that because you like T—Mr Burgess?'

'Yes. But there's another reason.'

'What is it?'

This was my chance to tell her the truth. It was not easy, but at last I said it.

'Because I like you.'

She smiled beautifully and said, 'That's a very sweet thought.'

She stopped suddenly. There were two paths in front of us. One of them went to the back of the house; the other led to the front.

'Which way are you going?' she asked.

'I'm going with you, to the front.'

Her face looked dark. 'I don't think I'll go,' she said. 'I'm tired. Tell them that you couldn't find me.'

'Oh, no!' I exclaimed. 'They'll be very disappointed.' I would be disappointed, too, because I had promised to bring her alive or dead.

'Then I suppose I must go,' she said. 'But I'd like to go alone if you don't object.'

I objected very much, but I did not tell her so. 'But you'll say that I sent you, I hope.'

'Perhaps I will,' she said.

Chapter 9

The next day was Tuesday. Between Tuesday and Saturday I carried three letters from Marian to Ted Burgess. I brought back one note to her and two ordinary messages.

When he had read her first letter, he said: 'Tell her it's all right.' The second time he said, 'Tell her I can't arrange it.'

He usually worked in the fields, and it was easy to find him. On Wednesday he was riding on a new machine which cut the corn. He stopped the horse and I gave him the letter. By Thursday afternoon he had cut most of the corn, and another man was on the machine. With his gun ready, Ted Burgess was waiting for the small animals which would soon run out of the corn. This was so exciting that I almost forgot about the letter. But we were both disappointed. The machine finished the work, and nothing ran out.

I gave him the envelope, and he opened it immediately. I knew then that he must have shot something. A thin stream of blood appeared on the envelope and on the letter. He had killed something before I arrived; and the blood was still on his hands.

I cried, 'Oh, don't do that!' But he was so interested in the letter

The blood was still on his hands.

that he did not answer.

The next day I found him near the straw stack, and he gave me the note.

'There's no blood on this one,' he said.

I laughed, and he laughed, too. I was not afraid of an animal's blood. I knew that hunting and shooting were part of a man's life. One day I hoped to enjoy those sports myself.

I had a lot of fun on the straw stack. I slid down it on each of the occasions when I took him letters. It was the best thing at Black Farm. Then, when I returned to the Hall, I did not have to tell a lie. I said that I had been playing on Farmer Burgess's straw stack.

They were wonderful afternoons in another way, too. As the messenger of the gods I was very serious about my duties. I was employed in secret affairs. Also, I was doing something for Marian which no other person could do. She talked a lot to her friends; she smiled a lot at Lord Trimingham. She sat next to Lord Trimingham at meals and walked with him outside. But when she gave me the letters, her manner was quite different. She was excited then, even anxious. She was never excited when she was with Lord Trimingham.

53

My services to Marian gave me great pleasure, but they were also a puzzle. I did not understand why the messages were important. And I did not know what they contained. Marian and Ted Burgess both said that they were 'business letters'. In my mind 'business' was a very solemn thing. It used to frighten my mother sometimes. It was connected with the long hours that my father had to stay in his office. Business was the way in which a man earned money. Marian did not need to earn money, but Ted Burgess did. Perhaps she was helping him. Perhaps the letters contained advice which brought profit to him. They might even contain cheques or pound notes, and that thought was exciting. Marian clearly had great confidence in me.

But I had never seen any money in the envelopes. The only things that Ted Burgess took out of them were short letters. Perhaps she wrote something that would be important to a farmer: something about the weather or the temperature, for example. I had not seen a thermometer at Black Farm. It had been eighty-three degrees on Tuesday, eighty-five on Wednesday and ninety-two on Thursday.

And then I had another idea. Ted Burgess might be in trouble, and Marian was trying to help him. I supposed that the police were looking for him. Perhaps he had killed somebody. I remembered the blood on his hands, and it might have been human blood. This idea was the one I preferred; but it did not really satisfy me. If Ted was in trouble, he ought to show some sign of fear. When I delivered the messages, Marian and Ted were both excited and eager. There was no sign of crime in the way they behaved.

I am ashamed now to say that I wanted to know the subject of the notes. Of course, I did not intend to open any of them. I was too proud to do that and too anxious to please her. But there was another reason: the truth would probably be a disappointment to me. I was quite right about that.

Friday was the day before the cricket match, and two things happened. The first was that Marcus got up. He was not allowed to go out. But Mrs Maudsley said that he would be well enough to watch the cricket match. I was very pleased to see him when he came to lunch. Although we were not great friends, we were about the same age. We shared some familiar thoughts, and I could talk to him without difficulty. I made some remarks about his spots, his pale face and his thin legs. He made fun of me, too. We sat together, insulting each other happily, and had a great conversation. And then, during the meal, I suddenly thought of the difficulties.

If Marcus was with me, I should not be able to carry any more messages. It had been easy during his illness. I was able to go and come as I pleased then. When anyone questioned me, I just told them about the straw stack at the farm. But that excuse would not deceive Marcus for long. He would slide down a straw stack once or twice, but he would not want to do it every day. He did not like pretending as much as I did. I was Mercury, the messenger of the gods; but I could never tell Marcus that.

I could not give Ted Burgess a letter, or take a message from him, with Marcus beside me. Indeed, he would not want to talk to the farmer at all; and he would criticize me if I did so. Marcus would certainly not go into the kitchen while Ted was slowly writing a letter.

The more I thought about the problem, the more difficult it seemed. Although I was used to deceiving people, I did not want to deceive Marcus. As I remember the difficulty now, it was not a moral one. I just did not want to lose a friend. At the same time, I loved the new spirit of adventure in my life. I knew that the loss of it would be a great disappointment to me. My services to Marian were now the most attractive part of life at Brandham Hall. It would be difficult to tell her that I must stop taking her messages. By the end of the meal I had almost stopped talking to Marcus. I did not know what was going to happen. Marian usually gave me the letters in the morning. But she had not given me one that day. After lunch, when Marcus and I were about to run away, Marian called me.

'Don't wait for me,' I said to Marcus. 'Marian wants to tell me something. I'll follow you in a moment.'

While he was hesitating, I went to one of the rooms. I remember shutting the door behind me. Marian was sitting at a desk.

'Marian,' I said. I was going to tell her about Marcus and my difficulties. But there was a noise at the door. She quickly gave me a letter, and like lightning I pushed it into my pocket. The door opened, and Lord Trimingham came in.

'I heard you calling,' he said to Marian. 'I thought you were calling me. But it was this lucky fellow. Can I take you away from him now?'

She smiled quickly and went to him.

When they had gone, I touched the letter in my pocket. I noticed immediately that the envelope was open. She had not had time to stick it down.

I found Marcus. I told him where I was going.

'Aren't you tired of that old straw stack?' he said. 'It's too hot to climb straw stacks today. Your suit will soon be very dirty, won't it?'

We argued a little. I asked him what he was going to do.

'Oh, I'll do something,' he said. 'I may sit at that window and

watch them spooning in the garden.'

We both laughed about that. We thought that spooning was the most stupid affair. Then a sudden thought gave me a shock.

'I'm sure Marian doesn't spoon with anyone,' I said, seriously. 'She isn't a foolish girl.'

'I'm not sure about that,' Marcus said. 'Some people think that she spoons with you.'

I did not like that remark, and I hit him. We fought for a few minutes until Marcus cried, 'Stop! You've forgotten that I've been ill.'

Pleased with my victory, I left him. I hurried away to read the thermometer. It was three o'clock. The temperature was ninety degrees and might rise higher. I hoped it would.

I was half way to Black Farm. I put my hand into my pocket and felt the letter again. With no other intention in my mind, I took it out and looked at it. There was no address on the envelope. I could see some writing on the paper inside; but I was looking at it from the wrong side.

I thought about the customs and the laws at my school. If a boy left his letters on a table or a desk, anyone could read them. It was his own fault, and he could not complain. But no one was allowed to take another boy's letters from inside a desk or cupboard.

In school we often passed notes round. If the envelopes were open, anyone could read the letters. But an envelope that was stuck down contained a private letter; it should not be read. The law was quite simple and clear.

The envelope of Marian's letter was open, and therefore I could read it. But still I hesitated. I was not sure whether Marian had intended to leave the envelope open. She had stuck down all the other envelopes but had given this one to me in a great hurry. I hesitated because she might have intended to stick it down.

But she had not done that.

At school we believed that facts were very important. Intentions were not important. A boy had either done something or he had not done it. A mistake made by accident was just as bad as a mistake on purpose. If Marian had made a mistake, she should be punished for it. But still I hesitated. I wanted to help her. She was not my enemy, like Jenkins and Strode. I was serving her, and her wishes were my wishes. I had to consider her intentions.

For a time I struggled with this moral problem. I wished that everything was plain and simple. Marian's face and figure came into my mind like a picture. And then I thought that perhaps she *wanted* me to read the letter. She might have left it open on purpose. Perhaps she had written something about me. If it was something kind, she would want me to read it.

I decided, then, to read it. There were other good arguments in my favour. This letter might be the last that I should deliver. If it was very secret or very important, I would probably carry more in spite of Marcus's presence. If Marian was in danger, she would expect me to read it.

But I did not take the letter out of the envelope. I read only the words that I could see. I knew already that three of them were the same.

> Darling, darling, darling,
> Same place, same time, this evening.
> But take care not to—

The rest of the letter was hidden by the envelope.

Chapter 10

The letter was the worst disappointment of my life.

I felt that Marian and Ted Burgess had completely deceived me. The adventure was thoroughly spoiled. It was just like a bad dream.

They were in love! She called him *darling*! I had tried to explain the letters to myself. But I had never imagined that Marian and Ted Burgess were in love. I had been a fool, and I felt quite ashamed. At the same time I tried to smile.

They had deceived me without any difficulty at all. All my noble thoughts broke into pieces. My arguments were torn apart. I had never expected that Marian would treat me in this way. She had been kind to me. She knew how a boy felt. She was my Virgin of the zodiac. I did not know how she could have behaved in this stupid manner. If she had been a young servant, I would have understood the foolishness. We were used to young servants who cried about love. They came to prayers with red eyes. But I thought Marian was different.

I remembered Marcus's remarks about spooning. He was probably right. I had no doubt now that Marian and Ted Burgess liked to spoon. Although I felt miserable, I had to laugh. I had almost worshipped Marian, and laughing about it did not seem right. I understood now why the messages were secret: she was ashamed of them. I shared her shame. I pushed the letter into the envelope and stuck it down.

But I had to deliver it to Ted Burgess.

When I left the shade of the trees, my thoughts became brighter. The sun was warm and kind and seemed to forgive Marian. Perhaps it changed some of my ideas, too, because I was ready to forgive her. I did not say, 'Spooning is a good thing because Marian does it.' I did not say, 'Other people mustn't spoon, but *she* can.' I was thinking of the other person. She could not spoon by herself. If she liked the other person—

I thought about Ted Burgess in a new way then, and I did not like the idea. But where was he? He was not in the field with the other men. I asked them where he was.

'He's at the farm,' they said.

'What's he doing there?' I asked.

They smiled but did not tell me.

I hurried there, thinking about the pleasure of the straw stack. It was one fact among a lot of doubts.

Ted Burgess met me near the gate and greeted me politely. I noticed that his arms were browner than before. He looked so strong that I envied him. It was not easy to connect him with spooning or with any other foolishness.

'Have you brought anything today?' he asked.

I gave him the letter. Turning away, he read it quickly and put it in the pocket of his trousers.

'Good boy,' he said. The remark surprised me; and he added: 'You are a good boy, aren't you?'

'I suppose so,' I answered. Then I said, 'I won't be able to bring you any more letters.'

'Why not?' he asked.

I explained the difficulty about Marcus.

He listened sadly, and his disappointment rather pleased me.

'Have you told her?' he asked.

'Who?' I was enjoying his disappointment.

'Miss Marian, of course.'

'No, I haven't,' I said.

'What will she say? She likes getting these notes. We shan't know what to do now, shall we?'

I was silent for a moment. Then I said, 'What did you do before I came here?'

He laughed and said, 'It wasn't easy. But she likes you, doesn't she?'

'I think so.'

'And you want her to like you, don't you?'

'Yes,' I said.

'You don't want her to hate you, do you?'

'No.'

He came nearer to me. 'Why not?' he said. 'Why don't you want her to hate you? Where would you suffer?'

I felt that he had put a spell on me. 'Here,' I said, and I put my hand over my heart.

'Ah, you have a heart,' he said. 'I thought perhaps you hadn't.'

I was silent.

'She won't like it,' he said. 'If you don't take the letters, she'll be angry with you. You won't like that, will you?'

'No.'

'She depends on them, and I do, too. They're not ordinary letters. She'll miss them, and I'll miss them, too. She'll cry, perhaps. Do you want her to cry?'

'No,' I said.

'It's easy to make her cry,' he said. 'You might think she was proud and calm; but she isn't. She used to cry, before you came here.'

'Why?' I asked. Perhaps she cried because she was in love with him.

'Why?' he repeated. 'You wouldn't believe me if I told you.'

'Did you make her cry?' I asked. I could hardly believe that anyone would do that. And I remembered that she called him *darling*.

'I did, but I didn't do it on purpose,' he said. 'You think I'm a rough fellow. And perhaps I am. But she cried when she couldn't meet me.'

'How do you know?' I asked.

'Because she cried when she did meet me. Isn't that clear?'

It was not very clear to me. But Marian had cried, and the thought brought tears to my own eyes. I began to tremble slightly.

He noticed this and said: 'You've walked a long way, and it's hot today. Come into the house.'

I did not want to go into the house. The kitchen was bare and uncomfortable. If we had an argument, that kitchen would give Ted an advantage over me. He was used to its ugliness, but I was not.

I tried to think of an easy subject of conversation. 'You aren't working in the field today,' I said.

'I was,' he replied. 'I came back to see Smiler. She's one of my horses.'

'Oh, is she ill?' I asked.

'She's going to have a foal.'

'Oh, I understand,' I said. But I did not understand. Babies were a great mystery to me. Several boys at school had claimed that they understood the facts about babies. They had offered to explain them to me. Perhaps Ted Burgess would explain them.

'Why is she having one?' I asked.

'It's natural, I suppose,' he said. 'Horses have foals.'

'But does she want to have one if it makes her ill?'

'She hasn't any choice,' he said. 'She has to have it.'

'Why? What made her have one?'

The farmer laughed. 'She's been spooning,' he said.

Spooning! The word struck me like a blow. When horses spooned, the result was a foal. I could not understand it at all, and I felt quite ashamed.

'I didn't know that horses could spoon,' I said.

'Oh yes, they can.'

'But spooning is very—*stupid*,' I said. 'And animals aren't stupid.'

'You'll understand when you're older,' he replied, quietly. 'Spooning isn't foolish. It's a word that nasty people say when—' He stopped.

'Yes?' I urged him to continue.

'When they're jealous. They'd like to do it themselves.'

'If you spoon with someone, will you marry that person?' I asked.

'Yes, usually.'

'Can you spoon with someone without getting married?'

'Do you mean me?' he said.

'You, or anyone.' I was chiefly interested in him, of course.

'Yes, I suppose so,' he said.

'Is it necessary to spoon with someone before you can marry that person?' I asked.

'It isn't necessary,' he said, 'but spooning is a natural thing. It's a sign of love.'

'Is it worse to spoon without getting married?'

'Some people think so, but I don't,' he said.

'Can you be in love with someone and not spoon?' I asked.

He shook his head. 'It wouldn't be natural.'

Ted Burgess was fond of the word 'natural'. If something was natural, it was right. At least, that was what Ted believed. And now I understood that spooning was natural! I had never thought of that before. I had always thought that spooning was a kind of game.

'If you spoon with someone, will that person have a baby?'

The question gave him a shock, and his red face became even

61

redder. I could hear his breathing.

'Of course not,' he said. 'What made you think that?'

'You did. You said that Smiler had been spooning. And that was why she was going to have a foal.'

'You're clever, aren't you?' he said. And I knew that he was trying to think of an answer. Then he said, 'Horses aren't the same as people.'

'Why aren't they the same?' I demanded.

He had to think hard again.

'Nature treats animals in a different way,' he said.

Nature again! His answer did not satisfy me. There was something that he had not told me; and I said so.

'That's enough questions for one day,' he said.

'But you haven't answered them,' I argued. 'You've hardly told me *anything*.'

'And I don't think I will,' he said. 'I don't want to put ideas into your head. You'll learn everything soon.'

'But if spooning is a nice thing—'

'Yes, it is nice,' he agreed. 'But you shouldn't do it before you're ready.'

'I'm ready now,' I said.

He laughed then, and his face changed.

'You're a big boy, I know. How old did you say you were?'

'I shall be thirteen on Friday the 27th.'

'Good. I'll make a bargain with you. I'll tell you all about spooning if you—' He paused then. I had already guessed the details of the bargain, but he expected some help from me.

I said, 'Yes, if I—?'

'If you go on carrying our letters.'

I agreed. The reason seemed clear to me now. I had learned a little about the force that drew Marian and Ted Burgess together. Although I did not understand it, I knew that it was strong. And its strength contained something beautiful and mysterious that I enjoyed.

Of course, I also wanted to find out about spooning; and I would not forget Ted's bribe. I was sure that I could overcome the difficulties about Marcus.

'You've forgotten something,' the farmer said suddenly.

'What?'

'The straw stack.'

He was right. I had forgotten it. It seemed to represent something for which I had suddenly grown too old. I did not want to play.

'Slide down that while I'm writing my letter,' he said.

Chapter 11

I was disappointed with the temperature on Saturday. It was only seventy-eight degrees, and the sky was cloudy. They were the first clouds that I had seen at Brandham.

At breakfast everyone talked about the cricket match. A team from the Hall was going to play against a team from the village.

'Ted Burgess plays very well,' Denys said. 'He's the man we shall have to watch.'

'Do you think so?' Lord Trimingham asked. 'In my opinion — and —' (I have forgotten their names) 'are more dangerous to us. Ted can hit the ball hard, but he hasn't much skill.'

Lord Trimingham was our captain, and he planned the game for us. But Denys was excited and soon spoke again.

'We haven't chosen our full team yet,' he said. 'We need one more man. Who is going to play?'

A few people at the table looked at me. I did not imagine that their looks meant anything. I was interested in our team, of course, and had wondered about it. But I had not helped to choose it.

'It's a difficult question, isn't it?' Lord Trimingham said.

'It is,' Denys replied. 'We shall have to reach a decision very soon. We must have eleven men.'

'What do you think, Mr Maudsley?' Lord Trimingham asked. 'We have to choose between two, I think.'

Lord Trimingham often asked his host for advice in this way, and it always surprised me. In other ways it seemed that Lord Trimingham, not Mr Maudsley, was the master of the house. But although Mr Maudsley seldom spoke, he never failed to answer a question.

'We had better discuss it in private,' he said. And all the men got up from the table and went into the library.

I waited outside in order to hear the result of their discussion. I had promised to take the news to Marcus because he was having breakfast in bed. I waited for half an hour before the men came out. I pretended then that I was passing by accident.

'Ah, there's Mercury!' Lord Trimingham said. 'I'm afraid I have bad news for you, Mercury.'

His remark puzzled me.

'We couldn't find a place for you in the team,' he said. 'Jim played last year' (Jim was a boy who worked in the house) 'and the year before. He plays well, too, and we had to include him. Miss Marian will be angry with me, but it wasn't my fault. You'll be our twelfth man.'

His speech was a great surprise to me. There was no disappointment in it. I felt wonderfully happy.

'Twelfth man!' I cried. 'So I shall be in the team! At least, I shall sit with them.'

'Are you pleased?' he asked.

'Of course! I didn't expect *anything*! Shall I go down to the field with you?'

'Yes.'

'Shall I get ready now?'

'You can, but the match is starting at two o'clock.'

'Will you tell me when it's time to go?'

'We'll all go down together.'

I was running to Marcus's room, but he called me back.

'Would you like to take a message?' he said.

'Oh, yes.'

'Ask Marian if she's going to sing "Home, Sweet Home" at the concert.'

When I found Marian, I did not think about Lord Trimingham's message.

'Oh, Marian, I'm playing!' I cried.

'Playing?' she said. 'Aren't you always playing?'

'I mean this afternoon,' I said, 'in the cricket match. At least I'm twelfth man. I can help the team if someone breaks a leg or feels ill.'

'That may happen,' she said. 'Who would you like to have an accident? Father, perhaps?'

'Oh, *no*.'

'Denys?'

'No.' I must have hesitated a moment before I said 'No'.

'You'd like Denys to be hurt,' she said in fun. 'But Brunskill would be better, wouldn't he?' Brunskill was the butler. 'He's a very stiff old man. He'll break easily.'

I laughed at that joke. I could hardly imagine the butler running.

'Or Hugh?' she said.

'Oh, *no*, not him.'

'Why not?'

'Oh, because he's been wounded already—and—'

'And what?'

'And he's our captain, and I like him, and—oh Marian!'

'Yes?'

'He asked me to give you a message.'

'What is it?' she asked.

'He wants to know if you will sing "Home, Sweet Home" at the concert.'

'What concert?'

'The concert tonight, after the cricket match.'

The brightness left her face. She picked up some of the flowers that she was arranging in a bowl. She held them up and looked at them.

'They're not very nice, are they?' she said. 'It's the end of July, of course. They don't like this hot weather.'

'It isn't the end of the month yet,' I reminded her. 'Today is the twenty-first.'

'Is it?' she said. 'I've forgotten the days. There isn't enough time to think, is there? We have parties every day. Aren't you tired of them? Don't you want to go home?'

'Oh, no,' I said. 'Do you want me to go home?'

'I certainly do not. You're the best person here. I'm depending on you. How long are you going to stay?'

'Until the thirtieth.'

'That's very near. You can't go then. Stay until the end of the holiday. I'll arrange it with Mother.'

'Oh, I must go on the thirtieth. I promised my mother. She misses me.'

'I don't believe it. You can stay another week. I'll arrange it,' she said.

'I'll have to write to my mother—'

'Yes, of course. So that's all arranged. And the flowers are arranged, too. Will you carry the bowl for me?'

'Of course,' I said. 'But Marian—'

'Yes?'

'What shall I say to Hugh about the concert?'

She thought for a moment and then said:

'Tell him I'll sing "Home, Sweet Home". I'll sing it if he sings "The Flowers in Her Hair".'

I thought that was a fair arrangement. I carried the bowl of flowers for her and then looked for Lord Trimingham.

'What did she say?' he asked, eagerly.

I told him the bargain that Marian had proposed.

'But I can't sing,' he said.

He looked very miserable about it. I wanted to say something that would make him feel happy. So I thought fast and then said:

'Oh, it was only a joke.'

'A joke?' he repeated. 'But she knows I can't sing.'

'That's why it's a joke,' I explained patiently.

'Oh, do you think so?' He smiled weakly. 'I wish I was sure.'

Later in the morning I saw Marian again. She asked me if I had given Lord Trimingham her message. I told her I had.

'What did he say?' she asked.

'He laughed,' I said. 'He thought it was a very good joke. He told me he couldn't sing.'

'Did he really laugh?' she said. She seemed rather annoyed.

'Oh, yes,' I felt quite pleased. I thought that I had improved both the original messages.

Marcus and I were discussing clothes for the cricket match. I asked him if I should wear my school cricket clothes.

'Yes,' he said, 'but not the cap.'

'Why can't I wear the cap?' I asked.

'You could wear it,' he said, 'if it was a special cap, like the cap of a famous team. But it isn't. It's only a school cap. If you wear it, people may criticize you. They'll think you're proud.'

'Ah, but it may rain,' I said. 'I'll need a cap then.'

'It isn't going to rain,' he said.

We argued for half an hour about that cap.

At lunch all the men were wearing white cricket clothes. It was not the usual kind of meal. Everyone stood up and took some food from the table. Marcus and I helped to carry dishes and plates. Then we had to wait for the others.

I remember my thoughts while we were walking to the cricket field. I hoped that we should win. It was very important that we should win. Victory was more important than any other thing. The members of the team were all equal now. The butler and the other servants felt that they were equal to Lord Trimingham and to Mr Maudsley.

I received a shock when we reached the field. The team from the village had already arrived, and only a few of them had white cricket clothes. Some wore working clothes; others had blue or brown trousers. They did not have the smallest chance of success against us, I thought. Unless they were dressed properly, they could not possibly play well.

Most of the men already knew one another. The others were introduced by Lord Trimingham. I shook hands with many people whose names I forgot almost immediately.

Suddenly I heard: 'Burgess, this is our twelfth man, Leo Colston.'

Without thinking, I stretched out my hand. Then I saw who it was. My face felt hot and red, and Ted looked surprised, too.

He said quickly, 'Oh, yes, my lord. We know each other. He comes to the farm and slides down my straw stack.'

'Of course he does,' Lord Trimingham said. 'He told us. You should make him carry messages, too, Burgess. He's an excellent messenger.'

'I'm sure he can do many things,' the farmer said.

Lord Trimingham turned away, and Ted and I were left together.

'I didn't see you when I came,' I said; and I looked at his neat white trousers. They seemed to change his character.

'I had to stay with Smiler,' he said. 'She's comfortable now, and she's had her foal. You must come and see them.'

'Are you the captain of the team?' I asked. I could not imagine Ted in any lesser position.

'Oh no,' he said. 'I don't know much about cricket. I just hit the ball. Bill Burdock is our captain. He's over there.' And Ted pointed to a man who was talking to Lord Trimingham. 'Look, they're spinning the coin,' he said, eagerly. 'But it's no use; Lord Trimingham never wins.'

But this time he won, and we played first.

The game had already started when the ladies arrived, with Marcus. I was annoyed with them. They should have been ashamed of their lateness.

'It's quite simple,' Marcus said to me, quietly. 'They just wouldn't start.'

He went with the ladies to a row of chairs. I sat with our team.

I have never watched a cricket match since that day at Brandham. I know now that it was not an ordinary local game. Lord Trimingham's family had always loved cricket, and Mr Maudsley continued the custom. There was a big wooden frame which showed the score. Two men wrote the details on large score-cards, and we each had our own score-card. There was a big white sheet at each end of the field. The boundary was marked by a white line. All these things were correct, and therefore they satisfied me. The match was an important one. Our team represented the honour of Brandham Hall. It was a serious affair, the result of which meant honour or shame.

Many people had come from Brandham and from other villages to see the game. Most of them showed favour to the team from the village, although they also applauded our men. But in my mind they were all enemies whom we had to defeat. I was particularly anxious that Lord Trimingham should succeed. He was our captain, and I respected the word *captain*. I liked him, partly because he represented the greatness of Brandham Hall. And I enjoyed that greatness very much. Our score was 15 when Lord Trimingham played. He

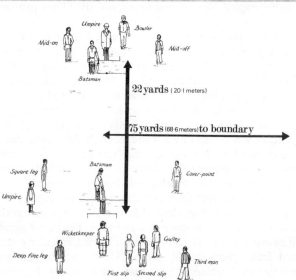

These are the main positions on the cricket field.

played beautifully for a short time but added only 11 to the score. When he came back, everyone applauded him. Marian's applause was louder than anyone's. Her eyes were bright when she looked at him. He tried to smile at her. I wondered whether she was secretly laughing at him. Her joy might be just another joke.

More trouble followed. We lost three more men, and our score was 56. Then it was Mr Maudsley's turn. He walked stiffly on to the field. He was then, I suppose, about fifty years old and looked to me like the figure of Father Time. I thought that he was clearly too old to play cricket. He reached his place and studied the positions of the other team. Bill Burdock and his men rubbed their hands and moved closer to Mr Maudsley. I felt very sorry for him. The game seemed to become a joke. Mr Maudsley could not possibly play for more than two minutes, and I waited sadly for his return.

But he did not return. He stayed on the field, and the reason is quite clear to me now. The qualities that had brought him success in business also brought him success in cricket. And the chief of these qualities was the quality of judgement. Sometimes he hit the ball, and sometimes he hardly moved at all. He did not waste his strength, but he scored. When a good opportunity came, he hit the ball *between* two of Bill Burdock's men. They were brought in closer; they were sent further away. But they could not overcome Mr Maudsley.

When Denys went on to the field, the score was 103. Mr Maudsley had made 28 of these. Before he went out, Denys had told us his plans.

'Father will get tired if he runs a lot,' he said. 'I shan't let him run. I'll either hit the ball to the boundary or leave it alone.'

For a time these plans succeeded. Denys hit the ball twice to the boundary, but he and his father did not play well together. Mr Maudsley was always eager to take a fair chance; but Denys often prevented this. Once or twice the crowd laughed at Denys's caution. We all noticed that Mr Maudsley was getting tired of it, too. At last Mr Maudsley refused Denys's signal. He shouted, 'Come on! Run, man!' The words were like a whip on Denys's back. He ran, but it was no use. The other team was faster. Denys walked back with a red face.

Mr Maudsley now controlled the game. Although I was pleased with his success, at the time something seemed wrong with it. It was wrong that a stiff old man should gain all the honour. Mr Maudsley was clever, and he possessed excellent judgement. But these, I thought, were hardly the right qualities for success in sport. I believed that strength and skill should defeat brains.

We quickly lost the rest of our team, but Mr Maudsley was undefeated. He scored 50, and our total was 142. When the men came in, there was great applause for Mr Maudsley. Everyone stood up in his honour, and Lord Trimingham shook hands with him. We had tea then and discussed the game. Mr Maudsley said very little. At five o'clock our team went on to the field. The village had two hours in which to defeat us.

Chapter 12

I still have my own score-card for the match. I knew all the members of our team and can remember every detail of their score. But I knew only Ted Burgess from the village team. I still have their score, too; but I cannot remember all the details. I thought that we should have an easy victory.

The village lost five of their men quickly. The score then was less than 50. The match became less interesting, and I began to feel sorry for the village team. My attention moved to the trees behind the field. I noticed the line where the trees seemed to meet the sky. There was a big cloud above the trees. The top of the cloud was round and white, but the lower side was purple. Was there some danger in that great purple part, I wondered. There might be thunder, but I did not think so. The cloud was moving very slowly towards the sun. As it moved, it became brighter and brighter. Soon it would reach the sun, and then—

There was a noise behind me. Ted Burgess was going out to play. He whistled as he went. I thought he was trying to cheer himself.

I was not sure whether I wanted him to score a lot for the village. I was puzzled because my thoughts had been quite clear until now: I wanted only our team to play well. But Ted Burgess was different. I felt some kind of loyalty to Ted. I wanted him to fight; and I hoped that he would fight hard.

He had a few narrow escapes, and then he began to score. He scored 4, 8, 10. He then hit the ball so hard that it fell among the trees. That knock added 6 to his score. A few minutes later he hit another ball to the boundary. Ted's score was now 20; and someone shouted, 'Good old Ted!'

I cannot quite remember when Ted's score began to worry me. It reached 40 and then 50; and he was still playing. Ted's 50 was very different from Mr Maudsley's. There was no judgement or care; it was just luck. But I knew that many victories have been won by good luck. I was worried and pleased at the same time.

Marian was sitting just below us, and there was an empty chair beside her. I felt so excited that I had to talk to someone. I went down to her and whispered:

'Isn't it exciting?' I hoped that she would understand my loyalty to the Hall.

When she did not answer, I repeated the question. She turned her face to me, and I understood. She was too excited to speak. Her eyes were bright, her face was red and her lips trembled. I was a child and usually lived among children; I knew the signs. The effect of the game on Marian was so strong that I felt it myself. I could hardly sit properly on my seat. Every moment the truth became clearer to me: I hoped that the village would win. I knew that she hoped so, too.

I looked at the score. Two men still had to play, and the village needed 21 in order to defeat us. The crowd was silent. Ted Burgess was still on the field.

We soon had no doubts about that. He hit the ball straight towards us. One of our men ran to stop it, but it was moving very fast. It struck his hand hard, and he could not hold it. Mrs Maudsley jumped up with a cry. Marian put her hands in front of her face. For a moment we were all confused. But neither of the ladies had been hit, and they both laughed at their escape. The ball lay at Mrs Maudsley's feet. I threw it to the man who had tried to stop it. He did not pick it up. His face was twisted with pain, and he was holding his left hand in his right.

Lord Trimingham examined the man's hand, and there was a discussion on the field. Then they walked off the field, and Lord Trimingham said:

'We've had an accident. Pollin' (that was the man's name) 'has twisted his thumb. He'll have to leave the field, and so we need our twelfth man.'

My knees were shaking when I walked out with Lord Trimingham.

'Ted Burgess is a nuisance,' he said. 'We've got to beat him. This accident has interrupted the game, and it might worry him. Now, Leo, you stand there. You won't have to do much because he usually hits the ball straight forward. But sometimes he hits on this side, and this is where you can help us.'

I felt weak and anxious. Five minutes ago I was sitting beside Marian. Now I was playing in the match. It was a very sudden change.

The game continued, and for a time no one scored. I began to feel calm. Then Ted hit the ball twice to the boundary, adding 8 to his score. The village team now needed only 11 in order to win.

Ten minutes later their last man came out to play, and they needed only 7. There was hardly a sound from the crowd. Lord Trimingham now had the ball, and Ted was getting ready to play. It was a curious situation: the tenant against the master, the farmer against the lord. But there was another fact: Marian. She represented the Hall and the master. But she seemed more loyal to Ted Burgess.

There was another great knock to the boundary, and the crowd cheered Ted. The village had now scored 140 and needed only 3 more for victory. Lord Trimingham ran up with the ball. Ted's face and body swung round, and he hit the ball hard. It travelled towards me in almost a straight line. Ted began to run and then stopped. He stood and watched me.

I stretched my arm above my head. The ball stuck in my hand, but the force of it knocked me down. When I stood up, I was still holding the ball. I heard the sound of applause. The men began to leave their places on the field. Lord Trimingham came towards me. I have forgotten what he said. But I remember one thing: his congratulations might have been given to a *man*.

I felt very happy. As my friends and others congratulated me, my spirits rose. But in one way I was sorry. I had made the catch which dismissed Ted Burgess. And I wanted to tell him that I regretted it.

I felt very happy, as my friends and others congratulated me.

I wondered how he felt about it. He must have been disappointed at the defeat of the village team. But I hoped that he still thought of me as a friend.

I went to him and said: 'I'm sorry, Ted. I didn't really mean to catch that ball.'

He stopped and smiled. 'That's a kind thought,' he said. 'It was a wonderful catch. I didn't think you'd manage to hold it. Indeed, I'd forgotten that you were there. Then I thought, "It'll go right over his head." But you stretched up and held it. I never thought our messenger would do that to me!'

'I'm sorry,' I repeated. 'I didn't intend to do it.'

The applause for Ted was very loud. He was clearly the favourite of the crowd. Even the ladies were interested as we walked past. All except one. I noticed that Marian did not look up.

I looked at the score-card. Ted Burgess had scored 81.

Chapter 13

After the cricket match there was a supper and concert in the village. The hall had been specially prepared for the occasion. Many local people were present, and both teams had been invited. The colours,

the flags and the heat all made me feel excited. The food was good, and everyone was very happy.

After supper Mr Maudsley made a long speech. This surprised me because he hardly ever spoke at home. It was quite a clever speech, too. He managed to mention and to praise almost every man who had played in the match. I was not very fond of speeches, but I listened eagerly to Mr Maudsley's. I hoped that my name would be included; and I was not disappointed.

'Lastly,' he said, 'I must mention Leo Colston, our twelfth man. Although he was the smallest man on the field, he defeated one of the greatest.'

Everyone looked at me. Ted was sitting almost opposite me, and he smiled broadly. He was wearing a dark suit and a high, stiff collar. He never seemed to look natural when he was dressed in good clothes.

The speeches continued, but at last someone said: 'Now let's have a song.' And there were general cries of agreement.

The end of the hall was raised above the rest of the floor. On this raised part there was a piano, with a small seat in front of it. But now I heard some whispering. The pianist was not there. His name was called, but he did not appear. Then someone explained: he was ill and had sent a message. But for some reason the message had not been delivered. There was great disappointment. A cricket match and a supper were not complete without songs. It was still early; the whole evening stretched in front of us. We already had a piano and needed only a pianist. Lord Trimingham looked at the faces around him; and everyone tried to avoid his eyes. Marcus knew that I could play the piano. I did not say anything but looked firmly at the floor.

Then suddenly someone moved. Someone stood up. It was Marian. To everyone's relief she walked quickly to the piano and sat down. She was wearing a pale blue dress, and she looked very beautiful.

The people who could sing had brought song-books and sheets of music with them. And Marian played the piano for them. She was an excellent pianist. Her playing was a lot better than their singing. The applause of the audience showed respect for the pianist and pleasure at the songs.

The members of the cricket teams sang first, and soon it was Ted Burgess's turn. But Ted did not seem to hear when his name was called. He did not move from his place. His friends began to encourage him, but he still refused to move.

'Come on, Ted!' they shouted. 'We're waiting for you. We know you can sing!'

Lord Trimingham spoke, too. 'Don't disappoint us, Ted,' he said. 'We didn't have to wait for you on the cricket field, did we?'

Everyone laughed then, and at last Ted stood up. He was not very steady when he walked to the piano. He was carrying a thick bundle of music under his arm.

The arguments had not seemed to interest Marian. When Ted reached her, she looked at him. She said something to him, and he gave her the bundle of music. Ted's first song started badly. Then, gradually, his voice gained strength, and he sang well. The audience applauded loudly and asked him to sing again. He and Marian said a few words to each other. Perhaps Ted did not want to sing another song. He bowed to the audience and left the piano. The applause then was louder than ever. The crowd liked his modesty and were determined to overcome it. At last they succeeded.

The new song was a love song. It has probably been forgotten now; but I knew it and liked it. And I liked the way Ted sang it.

When other lips and other hearts
Their thoughts of love shall tell—

The audience enjoyed it, too. I wondered whether any secrets showed on my face. I knew a lot about other lips and other hearts which told their thoughts of love. The song was a sad one, but it was also beautiful. The sounds of the words were like poetry. For Marian and Ted Burgess the poetry had a power which I could not understand. Although I did not understand it, I believed in it. I did not know then that love might ever cause unhappiness. It was a good subject, I thought, for a song or a poem. It was particularly good when the music was played on a piano. It was certainly not connected with spooning. At the end of Ted's song there were tears of happiness in my eyes.

The audience applauded Marian and Ted loudly. She bowed slightly, but he did not do anything. Everyone laughed, and Lord Trimingham said: 'He isn't very polite to her, is he?' The man who was sitting beside me said: 'What's the matter with Ted? He usually treats the ladies better than that. It's because she's from the Hall, of course.' But at last he bowed to Marian and thanked her. My companion said, 'That's better. She's a lady, I know, and Ted's a farmer. But they look well together, don't they?'

When Ted came back to his seat, he seemed annoyed. Everyone noticed this and enjoyed it. It added some fun to the party. Ted at a concert was just as popular as Ted on the cricket field. The crowd laughed at him as much as they had cheered him before.

Ted's first song started badly.

Other songs followed, and Marian showed us her skill at the piano. And then, during a pause, Lord Trimingham said: 'Now it's our twelfth man's turn. Can't you sing something, Leo? What have you learnt at school?'

After all these years it is not easy to remember my exact thoughts at that moment. Before the concert I had played in my first cricket match against men. That was my first test, and I had passed it. Now they wanted me to sing at a public concert. And I knew that I should succeed in this second test, too. I did not know that on my birthday there would be a third test. And I certainly did not know that my failing the third test would change my life completely. I had no music with me, but I knew several songs. I went to Marian at the piano.

She said, 'What are you going to sing, Leo?'

'I haven't any music,' I said.

She smiled at me, and I can still remember that wonderful smile. She said, 'Perhaps I can play for you without the music. What's the name of the song?'

'The Minstrel Boy.'

'It's my favourite song,' she said. 'I don't need the music.'

I knew 'The Minstrel Boy' so well that I did not have to think about the words. My thoughts wandered freely about the hall. Having no music, I could look at the audience all the time.

And while I was singing, the audience was silent. That was a good sign. It meant that they were enjoying the song. But the applause really surprised me. It seemed to shake the roof of the hall. I forgot to bow.

The people clapped for half a minute. They wanted another song. Marian was still sitting at the piano, and I went to her side.

'They want me to sing again,' I said.

'Do you know any other songs?' she asked.

'I know "Angels ever bright and fair", but it's a sacred song.'

She smiled again, but said: 'I don't know the music. I can't play it for you.'

I was very disappointed because I wanted to hear the applause again. Our conversation must have been heard by other people.

A voice said: 'Is it "Angels ever bright and fair"? I think I've got the music for that.' A man walked to the piano, carrying a book of songs.

Marian looked at the music and said: 'Do you want to sing the first part, Leo?'

'Oh, yes please,' I replied. I liked the first words very much.

> 'Oh worse than death, indeed! Lead me,
> Lead me to the flames;
> I'll thank your kindest mercy.'

I loved that song. I liked to imagine the kind of fate that could be worse than death. The Minstrel Boy had died in a war, and that was easy to understand. But something worse threatened the lady in this song. I could not guess her fate, but it always excited my thoughts. The song was a woman's song, and I was singing it for Marian. She was sharing the experience with me. We reached the second part of the song. And I imagined that Marian was floating with me in Heaven:

> 'Angels! Ever bright and fair,
> Take, oh take me to your care... '

Marian stayed at the piano, and I received the applause alone. But the audience did not stop clapping. She got up then and took my hand. She bowed to the audience, and she bowed to me.

After my success I returned to my seat. I was still excited by the angels ever bright and fair, and felt apart from the other people. Someone asked me if singing was going to be my profession.

'I would rather play cricket as a profession,' I said.

'Good,' somebody said. 'Did you hear that, Ted? You'd better take care of yourself.'

Ted did not say anything about cricket. But he looked at me and said: 'You sang very well. No one could have sung that last part better than you did. It was perfect. I thought that I was in church.'

That seemed to be the problem now. After my religious song, the party became quiet. It was late, and I felt tired. Perhaps I slept for a short time. The next thing I heard was Marian's voice. She was singing 'Home, Sweet Home'.

She had a beautiful voice, and the words of the song were beautiful too. I thought about my home and Marian's home. There were cottages and palaces, and they were both mentioned in the song. I wondered which kind of home Marian preferred. But later, I remembered that Lord Trimingham had requested that particular song. It may not have been Marian's favourite.

She refused to sing again. The applause that rang through the hall had no effect on Marian. Indeed, the harder we clapped, the further away from us she seemed. I was not annoyed about this, and the crowd did not regret her decision either. She was not like the rest of us. It had been a wonderful day and evening. Everyone felt satisfied with their good fortune.

On the way home Marcus congratulated me on my success. I wondered whether he was feeling jealous of it.

I said, generously, 'You might have had as much, or more perhaps.'

'That's true,' he said. 'On the right occasion I should have tried not to look like a sick cow.'

'On what occasion?' I demanded.

'I'm thinking of somebody who was knocked down by a cricket ball,' he replied. 'He lay on his back, with his feet in the air. And all the people of Brandham enjoyed the view.'

'I didn't. Oh Marcus, you're a—'

'You did. Then, when you were singing "The Minstrel Boy", you looked just like a sick cow. And you sounded like one, too. I was sitting beside Mother, and we almost had to laugh.'

These insults were perhaps not very serious, but they made me angry. 'If you weren't a poor, sick fellow, with legs like a bird's, I should knock you down.'

'Yes, yes, I know,' he said. 'I didn't feel quite ashamed of you.

Indeed, we were grateful. You got rid of that nuisance, Burgess, for us. When I saw him at the piano with Marian, I felt ill.'

'Why?' I asked.

'You'd better ask Mother,' he said. 'She hates the people from the village. Did you notice the smell in the hall?'

'No.'

'Didn't you? It was terrible. And then you sang that song about the angels; and that was terrible, too. I thought Burgess was going to cry. I couldn't guess Trimingham's thoughts because of his face. But he praised you. He told Mother you were wonderful.'

We were approaching the house. Marcus paused for a moment and then said quietly: 'Can you keep a secret?'

'You know I can,' I answered.

'Yes, but this is very important.'

I swore that I would tell no one.

'I'll tell you then, though Mother made me promise not to tell anyone. Can't you guess it?'

'No,' I said.

'Marian's going to marry Trimingham. Everyone will be told at the ball. Are you glad?'

'Yes,' I said. 'I am. I'm sure I am.'

Chapter 14

On Sunday morning my friends congratulated me again on my successes. I had won the cricket match for the Hall. My singing had been the best at the concert. I could not wish for more praise than I received.

But I was also pleased for the sake of Marian because she was going to marry Lord Trimingham. I could not imagine a better marriage. She was the most wonderful girl in the world, and he was the ninth Viscount Trimingham. It was an important affair; and it would have an effect on my life at Brandham Hall. Neither Marian nor Ted Burgess would ask me to carry any more messages.

I felt glad and sorry about the messages. Marcus was well again and might want to come to Black Farm with me. He would soon discover the secret, and I could not explain the letters to him. But I enjoyed the adventure and the risks. I liked Ted Burgess, too. Although he was only a farmer, I admired his strength. When I was near him, his strength seemed to put a spell on me. He was the kind of man that I should like to be. At the same time I was jealous of him. He had some power over Marian that I did not understand. I felt jealous because he, and not I, had that power. In one way we were rivals, but we were also good friends. And on that Sunday morning I was not worried by thoughts of Ted Burgess.

I am old enough now to know why. It was because I had defeated him. I had overcome him twice in fair competition. On the cricket field I had made the catch which dismissed him. And at the concert my songs had enjoyed greater success than his. The audience had applauded him, of course, but the applause was mixed with fun. They clapped for his singing and also for his mistakes. When I had sung, they clapped for the noble qualities of the words and the music. My songs of death and angels would be remembered after his songs of love had been forgotten. Ted Burgess had been very thoroughly defeated, and so he did not worry me.

I had almost forgotten his straw stack, too. I agreed now with Marcus: straw stacks were for young children, not for big boys. I even felt a little ashamed of it. Marcus and I could now enjoy the rest of the holiday. We could have our usual conversations and jokes. We could practise our own private fun. I thought of a few new insults for him.

I felt quite sure that Marian would now forget Ted Burgess. I knew nothing about love affairs at that time, but one thing seemed certain even to me. When a girl agreed to marry a man, she stopped writing love letters to another man. That was natural and right; no one could argue about it. My duties as Marian's messenger had been the most attractive part of life at Brandham Hall. But that did not seem to be true now. I felt jealous only of Ted's influence on her, and that influence had now ended. Lord Trimingham was hardly a serious rival. I did not think of him as an ordinary person. I wished for Marian's happiness. If she was happy, I should be happy too. Happiness was a simple thing, I thought. If you wanted something, you tried to get it. And when you got it, you were happy. I was sure that Marian wanted to get Lord Trimingham. When she married him, she would get his house, too. Marcus had told me that. And when he married her, he could afford to live at Brandham Hall. Marcus said that Marian would have a lot of her father's money.

After breakfast I wrote a long letter to my mother. I told her all about my successes. I also told her that Marian had asked me to stay another week. Mrs Maudsley had approved the invitation. She was glad, she said, that Marcus had a nice friend. I wrote that in the letter, and added: 'Please let me stay. I hope that you are not lonely without me. I have never been happier than I am now, except with you.'

I posted the letter and then waited near the door. The people who were going to church were not yet quite ready. I wondered what I should do in the afternoon. I thought of Ted and remembered his promise to me: he was going to tell me all about spooning. I had been very eager to hear that, but now I did not particularly want to hear it. I would not go to Black Farm in the afternoon. I would let him tell me, but not today. I was going to stay at Brandham for fifteen more days. Next week, or the week after, I would go and say goodbye to him.

As we were leaving the house, I noticed the clouds. I had already seen the thermometer, and the temperature was rising. It was going to be another hot day.

I soon felt tired of the prayers and again had no patience with the priest. He was telling us all to feel sorry for our wickedness. But I firmly believed then that there was *no* wickedness in the world! It was a perfectly good place, and so I did not listen to him. Instead, I thought about the Trimingham family, whose history was written on the wall. I had a special interest in it now because Marian would soon be a member of the family. Marcus had told me that she would be a Viscountess. And wives, I noticed, were included among the names on the wall. 'Caroline, his wife . . . ' and 'Mabel, his wife . . . ' were two of them. I imagined another: 'Marian, his wife . . . '; but I did not want to think about that. I felt sure that neither of them would ever really die. But even if they did, there would always be someone with the name Trimingham. The family would go on for ever. I imagined then the ninety-ninth Viscount Trimingham, and then the hundredth. In which century, I wondered, would the hundredth Viscount live? The idea of their unbroken history, for century after century, was a very solemn thought.

But it *had* been broken once. I remembered that the fifth Viscount was missing from the list. I wondered what had happened to him. Perhaps his name on a brass plate was in some other part of the church. And I decided to ask Lord Trimingham about it.

My chance came after church. Lord Trimingham was again last in the procession. I thought that Marian would wait for him. She did not, and so I did.

'Hullo, Mercury,' he said.

'Can I take a message for you?' I asked.

'No, thank you,' he replied. 'I don't think there will be many more messages.' His voice sounded perfectly content.

I almost asked him why there would not be many more messages. But I already knew the answer, so I said: 'She didn't leave her prayer book in church today.'

'No, she didn't. But have you ever known a girl who forgets things as she does?'

'I haven't,' I replied, 'but she plays the piano very well.'

'Yes, and you sing very well,' he said.

It was the praise that I had expected. And it was easy then to ask: 'Why is there no fifth Viscount?'

'No fifth Viscount?' he repeated. 'What do you mean? There are plenty of fifth Viscounts.'

'In the church, I mean. The fifth Viscount Trimingham is missing from the list.'

'Oh, yes,' he said. 'I didn't know you meant him. I'd forgotten his number.' He was silent then.

'Why isn't he in the list?' I demanded.

'It's a sad story,' Lord Trimingham said. 'He was killed.'

'Oh,' I exclaimed, feeling excited. 'In battle, I expect.'

'No, not in battle.'

'Was it an accident?' I asked. 'Was he climbing a mountain, or trying to rescue somebody?'

'No,' he answered. 'It wasn't really an accident.'

I knew that he did not want to tell me. Perhaps I should have stopped questioning him. But I was excited by my successes and decided to go on.

'What was it?' I asked.

'He was killed in a duel,' Lord Trimingham said.

'Oh, that's *fun*!' I cried. I was astonished that he did not want to discuss the fifth Viscount. That gentleman must have been a very interesting member of the family. 'What had he done? Did he fight the duel for the sake of his honour?'

'Yes, I suppose so,' Lord Trimingham said.

'Had someone insulted him? Had he been called a coward?—or a thief?'

'No,' Lord Trimingham said. 'He fought the duel about another person.'

'Who?'

'A lady. She was his wife.'

'Oh.' I felt disappointed. I suspected that the affair had been connected with spooning. But I tried to be interested and said:

'I didn't know that people fought duels about ladies.'

'Oh, yes, they did.'

'What had she done?' I was not very interested, but it seemed a polite question.

'He thought that she loved another man,' Lord Trimingham said.

'Was he jealous?' I asked.

'Yes. It happened in France. The two men fought, and the fifth Viscount was killed.'

'That was unfair, wasn't it?' I said. 'The other man should have been killed.'

'Yes, I suppose so. The Viscount was buried in France.'

'Did the Viscountess marry the other man?' I asked.

'No, but she stayed abroad. The children came to live in England, except the youngest. He stayed with her in France.'

'Was he her favourite child?'

'Yes, perhaps he was.'

'If the lady hadn't been the Viscountess,' I asked, 'would he have fought the duel?'

'But she *was* the Viscountess,' he replied.

'Yes, of course. But if they were only planning to get married, would he have felt the same?'

Lord Trimingham considered this. At last he said: 'Oh, yes, I think so.'

It seemed, therefore, that the fifth Viscount's position was not very different from Lord Trimingham's. But I tried to dismiss the idea from my mind. Marian was going to get married. I felt sure that she could not love Ted Burgess at the same time.

I said, 'Was he angry with *her*, too?'

'I don't think so,' Lord Trimingham answered. 'But he must have been worried.'

'Had she done anything wicked?'

'She'd been rather unwise.'

'But wasn't it her fault as well as the man's?' I asked.

'Nothing is ever a lady's fault; you'll learn that,' Lord Trimingham said.

This remark had a great effect on me. It agreed with something that I already knew.

'Was the man a very wicked man?' I asked. I didn't really believe in wickedness, but the word interested me.

'Several ladies had loved him,' he said. 'He was young and strong. — He was a Frenchman.'

'Oh, a Frenchman,' I said. That seemed to explain everything.

'Yes, and he could shoot straight. I don't suppose he was a wicked man. People were different then.'

'But would it be wicked if it happened now?' I was determined to find some wickedness.

'Yes. He would be a murderer now, at least in England.'

'Would the fifth Viscount have been a murderer if he had shot the Frenchman?' I asked.

'He would be if it happened now,' Lord Trimingham said.

'That doesn't seem fair,' I said. I tried to imagine the scene of the duel. It would be a lonely place. There would be cups of coffee and two guns. The men's friends would measure the distance: fifty steps. Someone would give the signal. The men would shoot at each other. One man would fall.

'Did the fifth Viscount bleed very much?' I asked.

'I don't know. That kind of wound doesn't usually bleed a lot.— Duels are forbidden in England now.'

'But men can still shoot each other, can't they?' I asked.

'They shot me,' he answered, trying to smile.

'Yes, but that was in a war. Do men still shoot each other about ladies?'

'Sometimes,' he said.

'And then they're murderers, aren't they?'

'Yes,' he replied.

We had caught up with Marian. Lord Trimingham noticed her suddenly and said: 'Ah, there's Marian. Shall we go and talk to her?'

Chapter 15

I still remember that conversation with Lord Trimingham. One idea was new to me then and seemed particularly important. He had said that nothing was ever a lady's fault. No matter what happened, a lady could not be blamed. The more I thought about the idea, the more generous it seemed.

After lunch Marcus said to me, 'I'm sorry I can't play with you this afternoon.'

'Oh, why not?' I asked. I felt quite disappointed.

'I'm going to visit our old nurse, Nannie Robson, who lives in the village. She isn't very well. Marian asked me to stay with her for the afternoon; and I suppose I must go. Marian said that she's going there, too, after tea.'

'Will you tell Nannie Robson about Marian and Lord Trimingham?' I asked.

'No, of course not. It's still a secret. And you mustn't tell anyone, either. But what are you going to do? You're not going back to that old straw stack, are you?'

'Oh no,' I replied. 'I'm tired of that. I might go down to the rubbish heap and then—'

'That's your proper place,' he said in fun. 'You're a bit of rubbish yourself.'

We had a little fight before he left me.

I had not visited the rubbish heap for more than a week. I liked wandering about there. It was a pile of old things that had been thrown out of the house. And I hoped to find something of value. But first I went to see the thermometer.

On my way I thought about Marian's kindness to her old nurse. It was another part of her character. She had been very kind to me. And now I knew that she was also kind to old or poor people. She really was a wonderful girl.

The temperature was eighty-one degrees; that was three degrees higher than it had been yesterday. The marker was still rising. I hoped that it would reach eighty-five during the afternoon.

My thoughts returned to Marian. I wondered what present she would take to Nannie Robson: a cake, perhaps, or a bowl of soup. And then a voice behind me made me jump.

'Hullo, Leo! You're the man I'm looking for.'

It was Marian, but she was not carrying a cake or a bowl of soup. She was carrying a letter.

'Will you do something for me?' she said.

'Oh yes. What shall I do?'

'Just deliver this letter.'

I did not think of Ted Burgess at all.

'To whom?' I asked.

'To whom?' she repeated. 'To the farm, of course. What's the matter with you?'

I was astonished. I could not believe the words that I had heard. Many thoughts rushed into my mind, but only one remained there. It was a terrible thought. Marian was going to marry Lord Trimingham, but she was still in love with Ted. And I knew what the result of that might be: somebody would be murdered. I felt really frightened and cried out:

'Oh, I can't!'

'Why can't you?' she asked in a puzzled way.

It was a very difficult question, and I could hardly answer it. I knew the secret of her letters to Ted Burgess. I knew that she was going to marry Lord Trimingham. I should not have answered at all. I ought to have run away from her. But I was very frightened. I believed that somebody would be murdered; and this fear made me answer her.

'It's because of Hugh,' I said.

'Hugh?' she repeated. 'What do you mean?'

'He might be worried.'

I saw her temper then. Her eyes looked very angry. She came nearer and stood over me.

'This is not Hugh's business,' she said. 'Only Mr Burgess is interested in it, as I told you before. Do you understand, or are you a stupid boy?'

I was so frightened now that I could not say a word.

'You are a guest in our house,' she cried. 'We have welcomed you and treated you well. I have been kind to you. You haven't forgotten that, I hope. And when I ask you to deliver a letter, you refuse! I'll never ask you to do anything for me again. Never! I won't speak to you again!'

I tried to stop her angry words. I raised my hands to push her away, or perhaps to bring her closer. She almost struck at me in her temper. Indeed, it would have brought some relief if she had actually hit me.

Then suddenly her manner changed, and she became very calm.

'Oh, I know your trouble,' she said. 'You want me to pay you, don't you?' She opened her bag. 'How much do you want?'

I had suffered enough. I took the letter from her hand and ran away as fast as I could.

I was used to criticism from other people. At school I had learned how to treat angry words. But Marian was different. In my ordinary life she had helped me in so many ways that I should miss her kindness. She had not laughed at my clothes when I first came to Brandham. She had bought me all my new clothes. It was because of her that I had enjoyed the greatest success at the concert.

But she was also the queen of my private thoughts. She was my Virgin of the zodiac! For many hours I used to think about her in various wonderful ways. If this quarrel ended her love for me, all my private pleasure would end, too. As I ran further from her, my sadness increased. The truth became clearer to me.

I understood now that she did not really love me. Everything she had done for me had been a kind of bribe. She had pretended to be fond of me, so that I would carry messages between her and Ted Burgess. Her kindness was not sincere.

The shock of this discovery made me stop running, and I began to cry. Crying relieved my disappointment. I crossed the river. There was no one in the field. It was Sunday, of course. I would have to go on to the farm.

I remembered then all the ways in which Marian had deceived me. She had told her mother that I did not enjoy the trips and the parties. She wanted me to go to Black Farm instead! For the same reason she had asked me to stay an extra week at Brandham and had arranged it with her mother. For the same reason she had got rid of Marcus today. It was not kindness to their old nurse, Nannie Robson. She had asked him to visit the old lady so that he could not go with me to the farm! I even believed that she had played the piano at the concert for the sake of Ted Burgess!

I cried again, although I could not hate Marian. I remembered Lord Trimingham's words: 'Nothing is ever a lady's fault.' It was a very happy thought. But the trouble must be somebody's fault. I wondered whose fault it was. And I thought it must be Ted's fault.

I soon arrived at the gate of Ted's farm. I waited there, hoping to see him. I would give him the letter and then run away, without speaking to him. But I did not see him. He was probably in the house.

I walked past the straw stack and knocked at the kitchen door. There was no answer, so I went in.

Ted was sitting at the table. He was holding a gun between his knees. He was so interested in the gun that he had not heard me. But when I stood beside him, he jumped up.

'Hullo,' he said. 'I'm glad to see you.' He laid the gun against the table and looked at me. 'Have you been crying?' he asked. 'Your eyes are red. What's the matter? Has somebody been scolding you? It's some woman, probably.'

I started crying again then. He took a handkerchief out of his pocket and wiped my eyes. I did not object to this. I knew that tears would have no effect on Ted's opinion of me.

'I must do something to make you happy,' he said. 'Would you like to see Smiler and her foal?'

'No, thank you,' I said.

'Would you like to slide down the straw stack? I've put some more straw at the bottom.'

'No, thank you.'

He looked round the room. 'Would you like to use my gun?' he asked. 'I was going to clean it, but I can do that later.'

I shook my head. I did not want to agree with anything that he suggested.

'Why not?' he said. 'You *must* learn how to use a gun. This one will hurt your hands a little, but it's not like a cricket ball! Ah, I haven't forgiven you yet for making that catch.'

When he mentioned the cricket ball, my resistance lost some of its strength. I became interested in his suggestion.

'Come outside,' he said, 'and I'll shoot something. There's a lot of birds round the farm.'

I could not continue refusing, so I followed him outside. I thought that shooting was a slow affair. We would have to hide and wait for the birds. But I was wrong. No sooner were we outside than Ted raised the gun to his shoulder.

The noise frightened me. I watched the bird as it turned slowly in the air. It landed just in front of us.

'That one won't eat my corn again,' he said.

He picked up the dead bird and threw it into some bushes. The other birds flew away.

'They won't come back for a long time,' Ted remarked. 'I was lucky to kill that one.'

'Do you ever miss?' I asked.

'Oh yes, sometimes. Now, would you like to watch while I'm cleaning the gun?'

I felt a lot better when I went back into the kitchen. Ted poured

No sooner were we outside than Ted raised the gun to his shoulder.

some oil on a piece of cloth and then cleaned the gun. When he had finished, he gave the gun to me. I held it up, pointing it at several objects in the room. Then I pointed it straight at Ted.

'You mustn't do that!' he cried. 'You must never point a gun at anybody.'

I quickly gave the gun back to him.

'I'll make you a cup of tea,' he said. 'But I'll have to boil some water first. Just wait a minute.' He went out of the kitchen.

He returned suddenly and said, 'Have you brought a letter for me?'

I gave it to him. I had forgotten it.

He put a cloth and some cups on the table. 'I'm alone today,' he said. 'The woman who cleans the house doesn't come on Sundays.'

Something made me think of Marian; and I wanted to go back to Brandham Hall.

'Have you any message for Marian?' I asked.

'Yes,' he replied, 'but do you want to take it?'

The question surprised me. I thought I was going to cry again.

'No,' I said; 'but if I don't, she'll be very angry.'

'Was it Marian who made you cry?' he asked. I did not answer, and he continued: 'We ought to give you something. A messenger ought to be paid. What would you like?'

I should have answered 'Nothing'. But Ted seemed to have put a spell on me again. He was not angry with me. There was nothing that we might argue about. Our conversation was perfectly natural. I wanted to please him. I did not refuse his bribe as I had refused Marian's money. And suddenly I remembered something.

'You promised to tell me something,' I said.

'Did I?'

'Yes. You promised to tell me all about spooning. That's partly why I came today.' It was not true, of course. Marian had made me come. But it seemed a good reason.

'Yes, I remember,' he said. 'But wait. I think the water is boiling.' He left the kitchen but soon came back.

'I enjoyed your singing at the concert,' he said.

'I enjoyed yours, too.'

'Oh, I don't sing properly,' he said. 'I've had no lessons. But you sang just like a bird.'

'I practised those songs at school,' I said. 'We have quite a good teacher.'

'I didn't go to school for long,' Ted said. 'When I was a boy, my mother took me to Norwich Cathedral. The singing was wonderful.

One of the boys had a voice just like yours. I've never forgotten it.'

I enjoyed the praise. But I suspected that Ted was trying to change the subject of our conversation.

'Thank you,' I said; 'but you were going to tell me about spooning.'

He moved the cups and saucers on the table. 'Yes,' he said. 'I don't think I will tell you now.'

'Why not?' I demanded.

'You're very young,' he said.

I thought about this and suddenly felt angry.

'But you promised!' I exclaimed.

'I know,' he said. 'But your father ought to tell you. It's his duty.'

'My father's dead,' I said. 'And I'm sure he never spooned with anyone.'

'Oh yes, he did,' Ted said. 'You wouldn't be alive now if he hadn't spooned. I believe that you already know all about it.'

'I don't, I don't,' I cried. 'But you promised to tell me.'

There was a pause. Ted looked down at me. Then he said: 'It means putting your arm round a girl and kissing her. That's all.'

'I know that,' I exclaimed, feeling very angry. 'Everybody knows that. But spooning means more than that. What else does it mean?'

'It makes you feel very happy,' he said. 'What do you like doing best?'

I was annoyed because I could not answer the question immediately. I had to think first. Then I said: 'I like doing the things that happen in dreams: flying or floating or—'

'Or what?' he asked.

'Waking up suddenly after a bad dream. I've dreamed that my mother had died. Then I wake up and she's still alive.'

'I've never had that dream,' he said. 'But it's the right idea. Think of it, and then add something to it. That's what spooning is like.'

'You haven't really told me anything,' I said. 'I still don't know what spooning is.'

'I have told you,' he said patiently. 'It's better than the thing you like best.'

I was too angry to notice how angry he was.

'Tell me about it. Describe it for me,' I cried. 'You know, but you won't tell me. I won't take any more messages for you unless you tell me.'

But Ted had no more patience with me. He stood beside me, as hard and straight and dangerous as his gun. I saw the temper in his eyes.

'Go,' he said. 'Go quickly, or you'll be sorry.'

Chapter 16

Brandham Hall,
Near Norwich,
Norfolk.

Dear Mother (I wrote),

'I am sorry to tell you that I am not enjoying myself here. When I wrote to you this morning, I was enjoying myself; but not now. I don't like carrying the messages. Please, mother, send me a telegram. Say that you want me to come back. You can say that I must be at home on my birthday. That's on Friday, July 27th, so there is still plenty of time. If a long telegram is expensive, just say: "Please send Leo back. I will write and explain." I don't want to stay here, Mother. The people are very kind to me, and I like the place. But I am tired of the messages.'

I paused then. I ought to explain the messages, but how could I? They were absolute secrets. Although I did not understand their reasons, Marian and Ted had both been very angry with me. I knew something about Ted's violence. I had heard his threat and seen his gun. That gun could kill, and Lord Trimingham would be the victim. I remembered the fate of the fifth Viscount.

I could not tell my mother these secrets, but I could use other arguments. She would understand how I felt. I continued my letter.

'The farm is two miles away. I have to cross the river and go along a rough path. I get very tired in the Great Heat' (my mother was fond of saying 'in the great heat'. She hated hot weather), 'and there are some wild animals which frighten me. I have to go to the farm nearly every day. They seem to depend on the messages. When I don't want to take them, they are angry.'

I could also provide some moral arguments, and these might influence my mother. When I did something wrong, she described it in either of two ways. It was either Rather Wrong or Very Wrong. I did not believe that anything was wrong. But my mother did, and so I wrote:

'I think that these messages are Rather Wrong. They may even be Very Wrong. I am sure that you would not like me to carry them. Please send the telegram as soon as you get this letter.

I hope you are quite well, mother. I should be very happy if I did not have to carry these messages.

Your loving son,
Leo

When I had finished the letter, I felt much better. My wounds had healed a little, I thought. In one afternoon I had twice run away from angry people. I had run out of Ted's house as fast as any boy could run. When I reached the gate of the farm, I looked back. Ted was waving and shouting at me. I thought he intended to run after me. So I kept on running until I could hardly breathe. By then I was over the river again. I was on land that belonged to Brandham Hall. Ted would not follow me there, and I felt safe from his gun, too.

But my pride had suffered. I had gained the victory at the cricket match; and I had succeeded at the concert. Ted Burgess had praised both these successes. I wondered whether my friends at the Hall would still praise them.

I quite expected that Marian would have told everyone about our quarrel. She would have told everyone that I was a stupid, ungrateful boy. She might even have told them that I needed payment for my help. I imagined that no one would speak to me.

I arrived for tea at the usual time, and everyone was kind to me. I was greeted and praised. Mrs Maudsley was not there. Marian was in charge of the table, and she seemed very happy indeed.

Her success in this duty was different from her mother's. Mrs Maudsley had always commanded the meal. Her guests seemed to eat and drink according to her orders. But Marian amused us. We laughed at each other, and we all enjoyed the occasion. Lord Trimingham was sitting beside her on a low chair. We could see only his head, but everyone could see her. It was a picture of the future, I thought. When she became Viscountess Trimingham, she would always be in the chief position. He would be beside her, in her shadow. I wondered where Mrs Maudsley was. She had never been absent from tea before.

Marian poured a cup of tea for me. She looked straight at me and said: 'Three lumps of sugar, or four, Leo?'

'Four, please.' I said it on purpose. I hoped that the other guests would laugh. And they did.

I thought of Ted's lonely tea at Black Farm. His kitchen was like the cage of some wild animal. Here, I was surrounded by wealth and comfort. Tea at Brandham was an exciting experience. I enjoyed it more, perhaps, because I knew Ted's poor home.

Later, Marian looked at me again. Although she did not speak, there was a clear message in her eyes. It was: 'I want to talk to you after tea. Stay here when the others leave. Or look for me.'

But I did not stay there, and I did not look for her. I went to my room, locked the door and wrote the letter to my mother.

I had decided to leave Brandham. When I left, the messages between Marian and Ted would have to stop. There was no other person who might carry them. If there were no messages, Marian would not be able to meet Ted. And then they could hardly remain friends. She would have to stop loving him. That was right and fair.

I had once liked being their messenger, but now I hated it. It was wrong. The letters were still the same, but I had changed. It was the first time that other people's business had ever worried me. If anyone attacked me at school, I would defend myself. If I did anything wrong, I would try to avoid punishment. Other boys could do anything they wished. It was not my business. But now I was anxious to interfere between Marian and Ted. I wanted to prevent their love.

Although they had both annoyed me, it was not really their fault. I had to be fair. I had attacked them first, and they were defending themselves against me. I knew the best remedy for myself: I had to leave Brandham Hall. It was also the best remedy for Marian and Ted; and for Lord Trimingham.

As I was going to post the letter, Lord Trimingham called me.

'Would you like to do something for me?' he said.

'Oh, yes!'

'Find Marian, please.'

I felt weak. I did not want to see Marian at all.

'But you told me that there would not be any more messages!' I said.

He seemed to be annoyed. I thought he was going to be angry.

'Oh, don't worry, then. I wanted to say something to her. She's going to London tomorrow, and I may not have another chance.'

'Is she going to London? She hasn't told me about it,' I said.

'She's very busy,' he said. 'Please try to find her.'

I suddenly remembered a splendid excuse. 'Marcus told me that she was going to visit Nannie Robson after tea.'

'Nannie Robson is a nuisance!' he exclaimed. 'Marian is always there. She says that the old lady can't remember anything now. She even forgets whether Marian has visited her or not.'

I ran away then, but Lord Trimingham called me back. 'Don't run far in this heat,' he said. 'You look pale. I hope you're not going to be ill. We don't want two sick people in the house.'

'Oh, who's the other one?' I asked.

'Mrs Maudsley. But you'd better not talk about it.'

I wondered why I should not talk about it. Perhaps the family did not want the other guests to know that Mrs Maudsley was ill.

'Is she *very* ill?' I asked. No one had mentioned it during tea, and Mrs Maudsley had seemed quite well at lunch-time.

'No, I don't think so,' he said. He seemed sorry then that he had told me about it.

I wondered whether she was just pretending to be ill. People sometimes did that when they were annoyed. Perhaps Mrs Maudsley wanted Marian to go to London, but Marian did not want to go. The two of them did not often agree about their plans. At Brandham differences of opinion were usually between Marian and her mother.

Chapter 17

On my way to the rubbish heap I met Marcus. He asked me where I was going. When I told him, he said:

'Let's not go there. It isn't a very nice place.'

'Shall we go and see those old huts again?' I asked.

'That's a good idea. What shall we do there?'

'We can look at the deadly nightshade,' I said.

'Ah, yes, the Belladonna.'

'Atropa Belladonna,' I said. I could not often correct Marcus. But when he gave me a chance, I always took it.

The huts were at the end of the garden. We had to walk about half a mile. There were big bushes on both sides of the path. Sometimes the darkness there frightened me. Perhaps that was why the place attracted me. Several times I had begun to walk along that path, intending to visit the deadly nightshade. But I had always turned back. Only once had I ever seen anyone there; and that was Marian. But Marcus was with me now, and I did not feel afraid.

Suddenly Marcus stopped. 'Look at that footprint,' he said.

We bent down and examined the ground. The earth on the surface was very dry, like powder. The mark was quite small.

'I think it's a woman's footprint,' I said.

'Or a thief's,' Marcus said. 'I'll tell Mother that we've seen a strange footprint on the path. She's afraid of thieves.'

I was surprised that Marcus should want to tell his mother about the footprint.

'Is she?' I asked. 'I thought she was very brave. I'm sure she's braver than my mother.' I could not believe that Mrs Maudsley was afraid of anyone.

'Oh, you're wrong,' he said. 'She's often frightened. It's almost like an illness. She's ill now. She's so worried that she becomes ill.'

'What's worrying her?' I asked. 'The servants do all the work, don't they?' It was the work of the house that always worried my mother.

He shook his head mysteriously. 'It's Marian,' he said.

'Marian?' I repeated. 'But why?' Perhaps I was right, and Mrs Maudsley *had* quarrelled with her daughter.

'Mother isn't sure that Marian wants to marry Trimingham.'

That news astonished me. I had never imagined that she would *not* marry him. I was also surprised that Marcus had told me. I wondered whether he knew or suspected Marian's secret. If he knew anything about it, then of course his mother knew it, too.

Marcus was certainly her favourite child. She was not very fond of Denys, and she did not often speak to Mr Maudsley. Perhaps she told Marcus of all her troubles. My mother sometimes told me her problems, and they surprised me. Perhaps all women liked to share their doubts and difficulties.

A sudden thought came into my mind. 'Did you see Marian at Nannie Robson's house?' I asked.

'No,' he replied. 'She hadn't arrived when I left. The old lady was disappointed. She said that Marian hardly ever came to see her.'

'Lord Trimingham told me something that Marian had said. She said that Nannie Robson couldn't remember anything. She couldn't even remember Marian's visits.'

Marcus laughed. 'That's nonsense,' he said. 'Nannie Robson's memory is better than mine. It's about four times better than yours!'

I hit him then; but the news worried me. Perhaps Nannie Robson was right, and Marian hardly ever visited her. If that was true, then Marian was deceiving almost everyone.

I said, 'Lord Trimingham also told me that Marian is going to London tomorrow. Why is she going?'

'She's going to buy some new clothes for the ball. That's one reason. But she's chiefly going because of you.'

'Me? Why?'

'She's going to buy a present for you,' he said.

'A present!' I cried. For a moment I regretted my quarrel with Marian. 'But she has already given me many presents.'

'This is a special one for your birthday,' Marcus said loudly and clearly. 'Do you understand? You'll never guess what it is.'

I felt so excited that I forgot my fear of Marian's presents.

'Do *you* know what it is?' I asked.

'Yes, but I don't tell secrets to small boys.'

I shook him till he cried for mercy.

'I promised that I wouldn't tell you,' he said. 'And now I've got to break that promise. Swear that you won't tell anyone.'

'I swear,' I said.

'You must look surprised when Marian gives it to you. Swear that you'll look surprised.'

'I swear.'

'It's a bicycle.'

Bicycles are very common now, and most children have one. But in the year 1900 they were uncommon. I wanted a bicycle more than any other thing, but I never expected to have one. My mother would never be able to afford the money. I questioned Marcus about the details.

'I haven't seen it,' he replied, 'and Marian has to go to London to buy it. But I can tell you one thing that you haven't asked me.'

'What?'

'Its colour.'

'What colour is it?'

'It's green. And do you know why?'

I could not guess.

He began to laugh. 'Because you're green yourself, of course! Marian said that green is the best colour for you.' He danced round me, crying 'Green, green, green.'

I felt angry and disappointed. At school the word 'green' meant foolish or stupid. It was an insult, and Marian probably knew that. My green suit was also a present from her. All my pleasure faded away.

'Did she really say that?' I asked.

'Yes, yes!' he cried. He danced round me again and repeated the insult.

For a moment I hated Marcus, and I hated Marian. I decided to strike back at them both.

'Do you know where Marian is now?' I asked.

Marcus stopped and turned to me quickly. 'No,' he said. 'Do *you* know where she is?' He was suddenly very interested.

'Yes, I know.'

This was quite untrue. I did not know *where* she was. But I guessed that she was with Ted.

'Where, where?' he said.

'Not far from here,' I replied.

'But where, where?' he repeated.

'I don't tell secrets to small boys,' I said. And I began to dance round him, singing 'Little boy, little boy, wouldn't you like to know?'

When I had punished him enough, I stopped.

'Do you really know where she is?' he asked.

'Yes, yes!'

At that time I did not guess why Marcus was particularly interested. But the reason is quite clear now: it was a piece of news for his mother. Perhaps they had both suspected Marian's accounts of her frequent visits to Nannie Robson.

My attack on him and his sister made me feel better. It helped me to get rid of my temper. At the same time I believed that I had not really harmed Marian. I had only *pretended* to know where she was.

We had continued along the path, and the huts were quite near now. Suddenly I saw something which made me tremble. It was the hut where the deadly nightshade grew. And the deadly nightshade was coming out of the door!

The bush had grown so much that the hut could not hold it.

We stopped at the door and looked in. Marcus wanted to push past the branches and go inside. 'Oh, don't go in,' I whispered. He smiled and stayed beside me. From that moment we were friends again. We forgot our argument.

The bush had grown to a great height because there was no roof on the hut. Some of the branches had grown higher than the walls. The leaves and flowers filled every empty space. The plant seemed to have a secret power which might burst the walls. Its beauty was almost too dangerous to look at. The heavy purple flowers seemed to ask me for something which I could not give them. The bright black fruit offered me something that I did not want.

Other plants produce beautiful flowers, and they all delight us. Their flowers die, and then the fruit comes. But this plant was different. It had flowers and fruit at the same time. Some of its leaves were young and small, but the others were old and large. It was a very strange plant. Although I was afraid of it, it still attracted me. I thought that it possessed some guilty secret. I was very interested in every kind of secret. Perhaps that was why I loved it.

It was getting dark. The effect of the deadly nightshade was so strong that I did not want to leave the place. But at last I turned away from the hut. And at that moment we heard the voices.

One of them was just a very faint sound, but I recognized the other immediately. It was the voice which had sung at the concert:

When other lips and other hearts
Their thoughts of love shall tell—

I felt sure that Ted was telling thoughts of love at that moment.
Marcus did not recognize the voice. It was gentle but also urgent.
It demanded something but was also content to beg for it.

Marcus whispered: 'It's a mad man, and he's talking to himself.
Shall we go and see?'

Just then the second voice became clearer. But it was not clear
enough for us to recognize it.

Marcus was very excited. 'There's a girl, too,' he whispered.
'They're probably spooning. We must tell them to go.'

The suggestion really frightened me. I knew that Marian and Ted
were there. I did not want to see them at all, and I did not want them
to see me, either.

'No,' I whispered. 'Don't disturb them. That would be bad
manners, wouldn't it? Let's leave them alone.'

I started walking back along the path. Marcus followed me, but he
still seemed annoyed.

'They're on our land,' he said. 'Why should they come here to
spoon? I think I'll tell Mother.'

'Oh, don't tell her,' I said quickly. 'Promise you won't, please.'

But he refused to promise and probably told her that night.

We walked on towards the house. I thought about many things. I
thought of the duel that the fifth Viscount had fought in France. I
remembered the footprint which we had seen on the path. It was
Marian's footprint of course.

'When is Marian getting married?' I asked.

'In two or three months, I suppose,' Marcus said.

'Is it quite certain?'

'It's worrying Mother,' he said. 'But Marian isn't a fool. She'll
marry Trimingham.'

Then I thought about the green bicycle! If Marian intended to
insult me, I would accept the insult. And I would accept the bicycle,
too. It was already better than all my other possessions. If I went
home before my birthday, I would not get it. Mrs Maudsley and
Marian would be annoyed and would probably send it back to the
shop. Perhaps they would give it to Marcus, although he already had
one.

I imagined the scene when I arrived home with my bicycle.
Everyone in the village would admire it. I could not ride a bicycle
yet, but my mother would soon teach me. And then I would ride up

and down the hills . . .

But I was not very happy about it. I suspected Marian's presents now. The bicycle was a kind of bribe because I knew something about her secrets. She hoped that I would not tell them to anyone.

'You're very quiet,' Marcus said. 'I don't usually admire your voice, except at a concert. And I'd like to spit on all your stupid thoughts. But what has happened to your long, thin, snake's tongue?'

I did not answer because my mind was full of important thoughts.

I left him at the door of his room. There was plenty of time before dinner. So I ran down the double staircase and looked into the mail box. The letter to my mother was still there. It would not be posted until the morning. I touched the door of the mail box, and it opened. The letter was in my hand. If I tore it up, I should have the bicycle. If it was posted tomorrow, I should certainly lose the bicycle. It was a moment of great decision.

I pushed the letter back into the box. And I went to my room, feeling quite miserable.

Chapter 18

In the morning I looked at the letter box. It was empty. All the letters had been taken to the post office. I felt very glad.

Neither Marian nor Mrs Maudsley was at breakfast. Marian had gone to London by an early train, and her mother was still in bed. I wondered again about her illness. Marcus had said that her troubles made her ill. I thought that she always seemed very calm. But I was still afraid of the light from her dark eyes when she looked at me. She had always been kind to me, kinder, perhaps, than Marian had been. But even if she had been my mother, I should not have dared to love her. Marcus loved her, of course. Perhaps she was different to him. She always made Denys seem awkward.

I did not know whether Marian loved her. She certainly objected to some of her mother's plans, and this must have been plain to all the guests. They watched each other like two cats. But then they would also turn away from each other, as cats do. It was not my idea of love. I decided at the time that they did not trust each other at all. Everything seemed easy or natural when Mrs Maudsley was absent. I was glad, too, that Marian would be away until Wednesday. By then my mother's telegram should have arrived, and I should be packing my case. I already felt that I was not a part of Brandham.

Marian had been everything that I most admired. I loved the way she spoke my name. She had put a spell on me, but it was not just the spell of her beauty. It was mainly, perhaps, her quickness of mind. Her thoughts travelled further and faster than other people's. She seemed to know our thoughts before we spoke them. She often answered questions a moment before they were asked. But she never made people feel uncomfortable. She was very interested in people, but she had her own opinion of everyone.

Until yesterday I had loved Marian, but now all my thoughts of her were green and poisoned. I hated my green suit. She had always thought that I was green. Marcus had said so. It might have been a lie, of course, but I did not think of that at the time.

So I was glad to see her empty chair at breakfast. Today and tomorrow would be easy days. There would be no quarrels or unkind words, and I felt very relieved.

Four of the other guests had left with Marian. So we were only seven at breakfast: Mr Maudsley, Lord Trimingham, Denys, Marcus and myself, and Mr and Mrs Laurent. I remember very little about Mr and Mrs Laurent. The cats were away, and the rest of us were very glad. Denys talked a lot. When nobody wanted to argue with him, he argued with himself. He would not have dared to do that if his mother had been there. But Mr Maudsley never scolded him, except once; that was on the cricket field.

After the meal we did not discuss any plans for the day. There were no messages, no problems. We were all wonderfully free!

That day and the next were both very happy. They did not compare with Saturday and Sunday morning, when I had enjoyed great success. I felt now that I was getting well after a long illness. No one visited Brandham Hall, and we did not leave it. We did not have to talk or listen to anyone. I now had time to explore the house properly. On Monday the temperature was eighty-three degrees; on Tuesday it was eighty-eight. I hoped that it would soon reach a hundred.

'Marian will be roasted in London,' Lord Trimingham said. 'The heat in those shops is terrible.'

I imagined the scene: Marian was in a busy bicycle shop. Everything was covered with oil and grease. 'Oh, there's some on my skirt. What shall I do? It's a new skirt, too. I've only just bought it.' But she would not have said that. She would have laughed and made the shop assistant laugh, too. Then she came out of the shop. And the dust in the street was sticking to the oil on her skirt. Behind her I saw a small green bicycle; a new, complete bicycle, ready for the road.

A green bicycle! It was a splendid thought; but there was an ugly thought beside it. Marcus had explained the bicycle's colour in an unkind manner. If he had not done that, I might not have posted the letter to my mother.

My happiness now depended on the telegram. I hoped there would be two: one to Mrs Maudsley and one to me. I did not think that I should have enough courage to show mine to Mrs Maudsley. It might worry her and make her feel worse.

At breakfast on Tuesday there was a letter by my plate. I did not recognize the writing. It had been posted at the village of Brandham. I could not imagine who had written it. Only two people wrote letters to me: my mother and my aunt. I could hardly wait for the end of breakfast. When at last we left the table, I hurried to my room. The servants were cleaning the room. I felt very angry. But I had to wait until they had finished their work.

Black Farm
Sunday

Dear Mr Colston,

I am sorry that I sent you away from the farm. It has been worrying me. I didn't intend to send you away. It wasn't on purpose. I was ashamed to tell you the things you wanted to know. Perhaps when you are older, you will understand the difficulty. I hope you will forgive me. It was quite natural that you should want to know. But I didn't want to tell you at that moment. I feel sorry, too, because your father is dead. I oughtn't to have got my rag out, as I do sometimes.

I ran after you to apologize. Perhaps you thought that I wanted to catch you. Although you may not want to come again, I'd like to see you. Can you come next Sunday at the same time? If you come, I'll try to tell you. We'll shoot a few more birds, and you can have tea with me. I'm sorry you missed your tea here today. I hope they kept some for you at the Hall.

Please believe that I am sorry for my temper. And try to forgive me.

Your good friend
Ted

I read the letter several times. And I almost believed that Ted was sincere. But I had been deceived before, and I still suspected a trick. He wanted me to go on carrying the notes. I had been deceived before. Ted was ashamed to tell me about spooning. But he had *not* been ashamed to use it as a bribe. The letter had come too late to have any effect. I still wanted to know the real facts about spooning. But next Sunday I should be at home with my mother.

An older person would know that the letter needed an answer. But I did not think of it. I believed that a letter was a present. There was one sentence in it that puzzled me: '*I oughtn't to have got my rag out, as I do sometimes.*' I decided to look for Lord Trimingham and ask him about it.

I found him in a room which was called the 'smoking-room'. The men went there to smoke after meals.

'Hullo,' he said. 'Have you started smoking?'

'No,' I said, 'but I'd like to ask you a question. Do you know anything about Ted Burgess?'

'Yes,' he said. 'Why?' He seemed surprised.

'I was wondering about him,' I said.

'Are you still thinking about the cricket match? You caught that ball very well,' Lord Trimingham said. 'But Ted is quite a good fellow. He's a bit wild, of course.'

'Wild?' I repeated. I thought of lions and bears. 'Do you mean that he's dangerous?'

'He's not dangerous to you or to me. He's a lady-killer, but there isn't much harm in that.'

A lady-killer: what did that mean? This was another puzzle. I did not think that Ted would kill Marian. I had been afraid of a man-killer. But that fear did not exist now. The danger would end as soon as I left Brandham Hall. The ninth Viscount would never know that I had saved him from the fate of the fifth. I remembered my arguments with Marian and Ted. I was important to them. I believed that I controlled their fates, too.

'What else can I tell you about him?' Lord Trimingham asked. 'He's got a quick temper. He's had a few fights.'

I then asked about the sentence that had puzzled me.

'What does it mean when someone says: "I got my rag out"? Is it about cleaning a gun? When a man cleans a gun, he puts oil on a piece of rag. Is that what it means?'

Lord Trimingham laughed. 'No,' he said. 'It doesn't mean that. I've just mentioned it. It means being in a bad temper; getting angry quickly and suddenly.'

At that moment Mr Maudsley came in. Lord Trimingham rose, and I stood up, too.

'Sit down, Hugh, please sit down,' Mr Maudsley said. 'Has this young man started smoking already?'

'Has this young man started smoking already?'

Mr Maudsley smiled at me. I did not say anything.

'We've been talking about Ted Burgess,' Lord Trimingham said. 'I told Leo that Ted was a lady-killer.'

'Some people think so, I believe,' Mr Maudsley said.

'It's his own business, of course.' Lord Trimingham looked at me quickly. 'I've been talking to Ted about the army. He'd be a good soldier. He has no wife or family, and he shoots well, too.'

'Yes, I believe so,' Mr Maudsley said. 'When did you last see him? Was it on Sunday? Somebody here noticed him in the park.'

'I spoke to him yesterday,' Lord Trimingham replied. 'I went to the farm. But I'd suggested the army once before. I'm not a very good advertisement for it, am I?'

He was referring to his wounds, of course, and he was probably trying to get used to them. He wanted us to believe that they did not worry him.

'What did Burgess say?' Mr Maudsley asked.

'At first he wasn't interested. He said that he was quite happy on the farm. He may have other ideas now. Yesterday he asked a lot of questions about the army.'

'Do you think he'll apply?' Mr Maudsley said.

'He may. I'll be rather sorry if he does. He's a good fellow. There aren't many tenants like him, but somebody has to fight the war.'

'He won't be a great loss to the district,' Mr Maudsley said.

'Why not?' Lord Trimingham asked.

'Oh, there's one quite good reason,' Mr Maudsley answered.

There was silence then. I had not understood all the conversation, but I felt worried by it.

'Is Ted really going to the war?' I asked.

'He probably will,' Lord Trimingham said.

I left the smoking-room then. As I was shutting the door, Mr Maudsley said to Lord Trimingham:

'Somebody told me that he had a woman here.'

I did not quite understand that either. Perhaps Mr Maudsley was referring to the woman who cleaned Ted's house.

Chapter 19

I expected my mother's telegram on Tuesday morning, but by lunch-time it had not arrived. My letter to her must have been delayed. The telegram would probably come in the afternoon, and I hoped to leave Brandham on Thursday.

Marcus and I were now good friends again. He had overcome his jealousy of my success. During the day we wandered about the park and we talked about school. We practised some new insults on each other. We fought once or twice. He told me many secrets. Although I did not approve of this shameless habit, I enjoyed the news.

He told me about the ball. It was going to be a splendid affair. He explained the things that I should have to do. He took a programme from his pocket and showed it to me. It was a list of dances.

'Everyone will have to dance,' he said. 'There are English, French and American dances. Some are modern, and some are old. The old dances are for the old people, like you.'

In the middle of the list there was the word SUPPER. Then there were more dances.

'Who will give the news about Marian and Lord Trimingham?' I asked.

'We may not give it at all,' he said. 'We may just let it *spread*.'

'Oh!' I was very disappointed.

'It will spread quickly,' he said. 'But you and I will be in bed. We'll have to go to bed at twelve o'clock. You are really too young to be awake after ten o'clock. And do you know what else you are?'

'No,' I said.

'Don't get angry, but you're a little green. *Green*. Do you understand?'

I hit him, and we fought again.

I knew, of course, that I should not be at the ball. I enjoyed the conversation because it seemed unreal. The ball had rather frightened me because I was only just learning to dance. I could not turn properly. But I liked to imagine the dances.

I did not think that I was deceiving Marcus. My plan was the best one for everybody, but it had to remain a secret. Marian and Ted were deceiving me. If I went on carrying their messages, somebody might be murdered. So I was quite sure that the messages were wrong.

Marcus then told me about the preparations for my birthday. They were an absolute secret, he said. When I heard the details, my conscience began to worry me. I regretted my plan, too, because everyone was going to give me something. The green suit and my other new clothes had not been proper birthday presents.

'Mother is worried about the candles for your birthday cake,' Marcus said. 'She says that thirteen is an unlucky number. Of course, everyone has to be thirteen once. We may get twelve candles and cut one of them in the middle. Then there will be eleven big candles and two small ones. The bicycle is the chief present, and Marian will give it to you at six o'clock.'

I closed my eyes and thought about that splendid bicycle. My old love for Marian returned for a moment. But it was too late to feel sorry. The telegram would come this evening.

We had reached the road to the village. A telegraph boy on a red bicycle was coming towards us.

'A telegram!' we both exclaimed. Marcus signalled to the boy. He stopped and got off his bicycle. I felt sure that the telegram was for me; and I stretched out my hand for it.

'Maudsley?' the boy asked.

'*Mr* Maudsley,' Marcus corrected him. I put down my hand and watched Marcus's face. I wondered what he would think about the news. I was still sure that the telegram was from my mother.

Marcus opened it. 'It's only from Marian,' he said. 'She's coming back by the late train tomorrow. Now let's go to the village.'

I had been wrong. My mother could not afford to send a telegram. She had written a letter, and it would arrive tomorrow. So I should have another happy day. Although I was still at Brandham Hall, my heart was already at home.

But the letter did not come on Wednesday morning. I was surprised but not very worried. Letters were also delivered to the Hall at tea-time. And I felt certain that it would arrive then. I wondered how I could spend the day. It was already very hot. I hoped that the temperature would rise to a hundred degrees. But I did not want to look at the thermometer until the afternoon.

This would be my last day at Brandham. If they wanted me to stay until Friday, I would agree. Perhaps they would give me the presents before I went to the station. I hoped they would. At least, I wanted the bicycle; but I should miss the cake of course.

When I was going away to school, my mother used to ask two questions: 'Have you forgotten anything, Leo?' and 'Is there anyone you ought to *thank*?'

Tomorrow I would thank everyone whom I ought to thank. There were Marian, Marcus, Mr and Mrs Maudsley and the servants. I imagined myself thanking them. 'Thank you for having me' were the usual words. I might have to thank them for the presents, too. I would prefer to thank them all at the last moment. When I thought about the ceremony, I felt quite excited. Goodbye, Brandham! Had I forgotten anybody?

I remembered Ted. He had not given me very much, but he had written to me. He was probably going to fight in the war, and that thought still worried me. I ought to say goodbye to him.

But first I had to get rid of Marcus. I could not say goodbye to Ted if Marcus was with me. I had an idea.

Mother had said that I might bathe. I had promised not to bathe unless someone was with me. This seemed a good excuse.

I found Marcus and spoke to him about it.

'Ted Burgess promised to give me a lesson in swimming,' I said rapidly. This was not true, but I had heard many lies. And lying is like a fever: it spreads to other people. Actually, Ted had offered to 'pay' me in some way. I explained to Marcus why I needed someone with me.

'I won't be away very long,' I added.

'Are you going to leave me alone?' Marcus said in fun.

'You left me,' I argued, 'when you went to Nannie Robson's.'

'Yes, but that was *different*. She's my old nurse, but Burgess is ... ' I did not know the word Marcus used. But it sounded bad. 'I hope he won't drown you.'

'Oh, no,' I answered.

'You may drown him of course,' Marcus said. He did not like

Ted. Indeed, he did not like any of the people of the village.

One of the servants lent me a piece of rope. I took my bathing suit and a towel and went down to the river.

There was one field in which the corn was still standing. Ted was working there. I did not go to him. This was my last visit to the farm. It was a special occasion. Ted must come to me. He was driving the machine, and at first he did not see me. Then one of the men told him that I was there. He stopped the machine and began to walk towards me. I went to meet him.

Before we reached each other, we both stopped.

'I didn't think you'd come again,' he said.

'I came to say goodbye. I'm going away tomorrow or Friday.'

'Goodbye, then, Mr Colston, and good luck,' he said. 'I hope you'll enjoy yourself.'

I looked at him. His manner was strange, and he seemed different. I remembered when I had first seen him in the river. He had looked as powerful as some wild animal. But now he looked tired and weak. He was probably about twenty-five years old. His face now seemed a lot older than that. I remembered the questions he had asked me on Sunday: 'What's the matter? Has somebody been scolding you?' And I almost asked him the same questions. Instead, I said:

'Is it true that you are going to the war?'

'Why?' he asked. 'Who told you?'

'Lord Trimingham.'

He did not answer.

'Do you know that Marian is going to marry him?' I asked.

'Yes.'

'Is that why you're going to the war?'

'I'm not sure that I *am* going,' he said. 'She hasn't said anything yet. I'll go if she wants me to go. My wishes aren't important.'

I thought that was a cowardly speech. And now, after fifty years, I still think so.

'You haven't told anyone about us, have you?' he said suddenly. 'It's only a business affair between me and Miss Marian, but—'

'I haven't told anyone,' I said.

He still looked anxious.

'She said you wouldn't tell. But I said, "He's only a boy. He might talk." '

'I haven't told anyone,' I repeated.

'We don't want any trouble, do we?'

'I haven't told anyone,' I said again.

'We're both grateful to you,' he said. 'Not many boys would have done it for us. I'm still sorry I shouted at you on Sunday. Every boy wants to know those things, and I ought to have told you. I know it was a promise. But after you'd sung at the concert, I didn't want to tell you. I'll tell you now if you like. But I'd rather not—'

'Don't worry about it,' I said. 'I know someone who'll tell me. I know several people who'll tell me.'

'I hope they won't tell you the wrong things,' he said anxiously.

'How can they? Everyone knows the same things, don't they?'

'Yes, but I'd be sorry—Did you get my letter? I wrote on Sunday and posted the letter that night.'

'I got it on Tuesday morning,' I said.

'Good.' He seemed relieved. 'I don't write many letters, except on business. But I felt so sorry that I had to write to you.'

A lump came into my throat. I managed to say 'Thank you'.

'You said you were going tomorrow.'

'Yes,' I said, 'tomorrow or Friday.'

'We may meet again,' he said.

He came close to me and stretched out his hand. He seemed to think that I would not take it. 'Goodbye.'

'Goodbye, Ted.'

I turned away from him and then turned back.

'Shall I take one more message for you?'

'That's very kind,' he said. 'Do you want to take one?'

'Yes, just one more.' It could do no harm, I thought. I should be at home before the message had any effect. I wanted to show him that we were friends.

'Tell her that tomorrow is no good,' he said. 'I'm going to Norwich. It will be Friday, at half past six.'

I promised to tell her. I looked back once. Ted was looking back, too. He took off his hat and waved it at me. I tried to take mine off but could not. Then I saw that my hands were full. I was carrying my bathing suit in one hand and my towel in the other. The rope was hanging round my neck. I had forgotten all about the swimming lesson. Marcus must not see my dry bathing suit. He would think that I was a fool.

Chapter 20

Mrs Maudsley was not at tea on Wednesday. She was probably still worrying about the candles for my birthday cake. I should be worried, too, if there was no letter from my mother. I did not want

to attend the ball. The long list of dances had frightened me, and
Marcus had seemed to enjoy my fear.

But my troubles soon turned to joy. My mother's letter lay on the
tea table. It was the order that would give me my freedom.

I did not hurry to open it. I talked a lot and ate more than usual.
I wanted to postpone the pleasure that the letter would give me. I
should have to tell Mrs Maudsley about it; but I hoped to postpone
that, too. I imagined that I was the centre of all her thoughts. I
believed that she would hate my leaving Brandham.

My darling boy,
    I did not send you a telegram. And I hope you were not
disappointed. I hope, too, that this letter won't disappoint you.

    Your two letters came at the same time, and at first they puzzled
me. In the first letter you said that you were very happy. You asked
if you might stay an extra week. I felt very proud of your
successes. Then, in the second letter, everything was different. You
said that you were not enjoying yourself. And you wanted to come
home. I have missed you very much indeed. I miss you especially
now because your birthday is near. If you were unhappy, I should
have to send you a telegram.

    So I went to the post office. But while I was walking there, I
had another idea. I thought that you had changed your opinion
very suddenly. In the morning you were happy. In the evening you
were unhappy. I wondered what had happened in those few hours.
You said that you didn't like taking the messages. But you had
enjoyed the work before. Why is it different now? You would be an
ungrateful guest if you refused to do this small service.

    It's very hot here, too, and I have often felt anxious about you.
When you go to the farm, will you remember to walk? Then you
won't get very hot. You've often walked more than four miles,
haven't you?

    You said that the messages might be wrong. How can they be
wrong? You told me that everyone was kind and good to you. I
can't imagine that they would want you to do anything *wrong*. You
are only *carrying* the messages, aren't you? How can *that* be wrong?
Perhaps it would be rather wrong if you refused to go. It would
not be *very* wrong. I'm sure they wouldn't be angry with you. They
would be puzzled. They would wonder what kind of home you
have.

    Of course the great heat is a nuisance, I know. Perhaps you
should explain to Mrs Maudsley that you feel tired sometimes.

(My mother thought that I was Mrs Maudsley's messenger.) Ask her *very nicely* if one of the servants can take the messages. I am sure that she will say yes.

Please try not to be disappointed about this. It would be a mistake if you left suddenly. They wouldn't understand. I have read your letters many times. I think your hosts are good people. They will be very nice friends for you when you grow up. Your father wasn't fond of social life. That may have been a mistake. I should like it if you had many friends. Perhaps we can invite Marcus here. But I don't know how we should entertain him.

I think we ought to be *patient*, Leo. The ten days will soon pass. I shall be very happy when you *do* come home. You are like me: sometimes sad and sometimes happy. A few months ago you were unhappy at school. Do you remember? Some bigger boys were unkind to you because you used a long word. But you soon forgot about it and were happy again. I hope that you are already feeling better.

Goodbye, dear boy. I shall write again before your birthday. I'll send you a little present. I'll keep the real present until you come back. Can you guess what it is?

With all my love,
Mother

Grown-up people often refuse a child's request. When this happens, the child cannot do anything. He does not know what to do.

My mother had refused my request, and I could do nothing about it. I did not know whether to stay in my room or to leave it. Should I talk to somebody or say nothing? I knew immediately that I could not talk to anyone. It was impossible to share the problem. I was like a Tower of Silence in which the bones of a dead secret lay. But was the secret really dead? No, it was not. It was alive and dangerous and might even kill someone.

Soon I decided to leave my room. I had to stay at Brandham, so I must get used to the place again. I wandered about at the back of the house, and visited the rubbish heap. Some servants passed me and smiled. They knew nothing about the trouble that might soon strike Brandham Hall. I crept behind bushes and trees and soon reached the front of the house. I could hear voices there. And I wondered if Marian had come back.

I did not want to be alone with her because she was the main cause of my unhappiness. Ted had frightened me more than she had. But she had hurt me more. I understood men and boys. I knew how they behaved. I did not expect that they would be nice to me. Schoolboys know everything about each other's characters. They do not practise good manners in order to hide their real thoughts. Ted was like a schoolboy. He would be angry at one moment and then suddenly kind. He did not respect me or admire me particularly. And I felt the same about him.

But I *had* respected and admired Marian. Indeed, I had loved her. She had been as kind to me as a good fairy might have been. In another way she had been as kind as my mother was. Both of them had now turned against me. I could forgive my mother. She did not know what she was doing. But Marian *did* know.

So I hoped to avoid her. Of course, I should see her at meals, and I had to give her Ted's message. I controlled the business between Marian and Ted. Without the messages, they would not be able to meet. If they did not meet each other, there would be no danger. I was determined not to take any more messages.

Marian was at dinner that evening. She had brought two new guests with her from London. She smiled at me across the table. After dinner Marcus and I went to bed.

The next day was Thursday. Mrs Maudsley appeared at breakfast and greeted me with kind words. She was sorry, she said, that she had neglected one of her important guests. She had been quite unable to leave her room. I looked at her, but I could see no signs of illness. Her eyes were the same. Her look was still as sharp and direct as an arrow. We did not feel as comfortable as we had felt for the past three days. After breakfast we heard her voice, and other conversation ended. 'Now, *today* we shall . . . '

As Marcus and I were going out, he whispered to me: 'The cats have come back.' I knew that he was referring to his mother and Marian. I was going to reply, but we heard a voice behind us: 'Marcus, I want Leo to help me for a moment.' It was Marian, and I followed her.

She asked me how I had got on without her. I said, 'Very well, thank you.' I thought that was a correct and safe reply. But it did not please her.

She said, 'Those are the first unkind words you've said to me.'

I had not intended to be unkind. I wondered how to express my sorrow. 'Did you enjoy yourself?' I asked.

'No,' she replied. 'I missed Brandham very much. Did you miss me?'

I hesitated for a moment. I did not want to say the wrong thing again.

She noticed this and said: 'Don't say "yes" if it isn't true.'

I answered then: 'Of course I did.' It was not true, but I wished it was.

'You think that I have a bad temper, don't you?' she said. 'But I haven't really. I don't like quarrelling with people.'

I did not know what to say. I wondered whether she was trying to apologize, like Ted. She did not usually apologize for anything. She did not say any more about our quarrel.

'I suppose you played with Marcus,' she said. 'Did you enjoy yourselves?'

'Yes. I'm sorry you didn't enjoy London.'

'You're not at all sorry,' she said. 'You wouldn't worry if I was killed in an accident. You've got a heart like a stone. And all boys are the same.'

I did not like the conversation very much, and I was puzzled, too. Was Marian serious, or was she trying to make a joke?

'Are men the same?' I asked. 'I'm sure Hugh isn't like that.'

'Why do you think he isn't?' she asked. 'You're all exactly the same: stones, big lumps of stone. You're all as hard as the beds at Brandham.'

I laughed. 'My bed isn't hard,' I said.

She was silent then. I thought that she was unhappy. It surprised me because she was different from other people. She did not really need happiness. She could be happy if she wanted to be. She could also be angry, sad or gay, just as she pleased. Perhaps I knew why she was unhappy now.

'Is Ted really going?' I asked.

'Going where?' she said. 'What do you mean?' Her voice sounded surprised, and that should have warned me. But I hardly noticed it and went on:

'Is he really going to the war?'

Her mouth opened, and she looked straight into my eyes.

'To the war?' she repeated. 'Who said he's going to the war?'

I had never imagined that she might not know. Then I remembered that Lord Trimingham had spoken to Ted on Monday. Marian was in London then. But it was too late to change the subject.

'Hugh told me,' I said. 'Hugh asked him to become a soldier. And Ted said that he might.'

The news was a shock to her, and her temper seemed to explode.

'Hugh!' she cried. 'Hugh! Do you mean that Hugh has persuaded Ted to be a soldier? Do you really mean that, Leo?'

I was frightened. But I knew that she was not angry with me.

'Hugh said that he'd spoken to him about it.'

'Oh!' she cried. 'Hugh *made* Ted say that he'd go.' Her face was white, and her eyes were like dark holes in a lump of ice.

'No,' I said. 'That's not right. Hugh couldn't *make* him do anything, could he? Ted's stronger than Hugh.' The argument was simple and faultless, but Marian did not agree with it.

'You're quite wrong,' she said. 'Hugh is much stronger than Ted.'

I could not understand that at all. It was just not true. But a new look came into Marian's face. She was still angry, but she also looked afraid.

'Did Hugh say *why* he wanted Ted to go?' she asked.

'Yes. Because Ted wasn't married, and he had no family. He also said that Ted shoots well.'

Marian's face changed again. 'He shoots *very* well,' she said. 'Oh, yes he does. Hugh wouldn't dare to do that. I won't let him.'

I did not know whom she meant: Ted or Hugh. She went on, almost wildly: 'I'll soon stop it! I'll make Ted stop it! Ted's a dangerous man when he's angry. He won't go to the war. I won't let him go. I'll tell Hugh—' she stopped suddenly. 'A few words would be enough.'

'What words? What will you tell him?' I demanded.

'I won't marry him if Ted goes to the war. I'll tell him that.'

'Oh, you mustn't!' I cried. It would be the worst thing that could happen. I imagined the fifth Viscount's body on the ground. He was dead, but the wound did not bleed. 'Hugh doesn't *know*, Marian.'

'What doesn't he know?' she asked.

'He doesn't know about the messages.'

'He doesn't *know*,' she repeated. 'Then why does he want Ted to go to the war?'

'Oh,' I exclaimed, and I felt great relief. 'It's because—because he's a soldier himself. And he loves his country. And he wants the army to be strong. That's why he spoke to Ted.'

'You may be right,' she said. 'If you're right, then Ted is foolish. And I shall tell him that.'

'Why is he foolish?' I asked. The insult did not seem right, and I was trying to defend Ted.

'Oh, because he is. Why should he have to listen to Hugh?'

Later I guessed what she was thinking about. She believed that Ted's conscience was worrying him. And that was why he wanted to go away. But I did not think of it at that time. My idea was to defend him.

'Perhaps he *wants* to go!' I said.

'Oh, he couldn't!' she cried.

I thought she was afraid for the sake of Ted. But I know now that she was really thinking of herself. I asked a question that had been in my mind for a long time. It was a rather stupid question and not very loyal to Lord Trimingham.

'Marian, why don't you marry Ted?'

For a moment her face showed all her misery. 'I can't, I can't!' she cried. 'Can't you understand?'

'But why are you going to marry Hugh if you don't want to marry him?'

'Because I must marry him,' she said. 'You don't understand. I *must*. I've *got* to marry him.' Her lips trembled and she began to cry.

When my mother cried, I could hardly recognize her face. Marian's face did not change. But I changed, because I cried, too. I remembered my first days at Brandham when Marian had had pity on me. She had rescued me when I was in trouble. She had gained success for me at the concert. When she cried, she was Marian of the zodiac. She was the girl whom I loved. I forgot that she had deceived me. I forgot that she had called me *green*. We cried together for several minutes.

Then she looked up and said: 'Did you go to the farm while I was away?'

'No,' I said, 'but I saw Ted.'

'Did he give you a message for me?'

'Yes. He said he was going to Norwich today. It would be Friday at six o'clock.'

'Are you sure he said six o'clock?' she asked.

'Quite sure.'

'Not half past six?'

'No.'

She kissed me then. She had never kissed me before.

'Will you still be our messenger?' she asked.

'Yes,' I whispered, but I had to look down.

'Good. You're the best friend I have.'

When I looked up, she had gone. We had both forgotten that my birthday party was at tea-time on Friday. I had wanted to be at home when Ted's message had its effect.

Chapter 21

After my conversation with Marian I felt happy. She was kind and generous, and I loved her. But I did not approve of her actions. I decided, therefore, to have two separate opinions of her. In the same way her unhappiness and tears did not belong to her position in the zodiac.

We had each asked and answered several important questions. Marian had respected my opinions. I felt pleased with everything, even with the thought of the green bicycle. Green was becoming an ordinary colour again. But my happiness did not mean that my affairs had improved. Our discussion of the secrets did not make them less dangerous.

What would happen when Marian persuaded Ted not to be a soldier? Ted had said that she must make the decision. She had said that Ted was dangerous. I knew that he had a fierce temper. If Marian encouraged him, he might—

That was the greatest danger. The fate of the ninth Viscount might be the same as the fate of the fifth. Lord Trimingham owned Black Farm and was, therefore, Ted's master. But I did not think that he would order him to join the army. I did not think that he would want to fight a duel with Ted.

Lord Trimingham's wishes were clear. He wanted to marry Marian. Marian wanted to marry Lord Trimingham, and she also wanted Ted to stay at Black Farm. What did Ted want? He had said that his own wishes were not important. I did not really believe that. He now knew that Marian was going to marry Lord Trimingham. And his conscience had made him think about the army.

I was afraid for the sake of Lord Trimingham. I cried with Marian. But for Ted I felt a great sorrow. He was the only one who seemed to have a real life. He had shown me part of his life and had treated me as a man. I felt nearer to him than to the others. I was just their messenger, their go-between. But Ted felt that he owed me something.

If Ted had asked me for advice, I should have told him to stay at Black Farm. Lord Trimingham had said that he was a very good tenant. He loved the place and his work there. If he went to the war, he might be killed. When I thought of Ted, he seemed too big to be killed.

I wondered whose fault it was. 'Nothing is ever a lady's fault,' Lord Trimingham had said. So Marian was not guilty. He had not said anything about a lord's or a farmer's fault. But no one could blame Lord Trimingham. He had done nothing wrong. It must be Ted's fault. He had invited Marian into his kitchen, and he had put a spell on her. I now determined to break that spell for the sake of everyone.

I had already begun to break it. Marian would not find him near the huts at six o'clock. Ted had said half past six. Would she wait half an hour for him? I did not think so. She did not like waiting for anything and would not wait more than five minutes. She might be angry with him. I imagined a quarrel between them.

'I'll never come again! I'll never come again!' she would say. And Ted would answer: 'I've often waited longer for you. I'm a busy man, and it's harvest time.' 'Oh, you're only a farmer. You can always wait for people.' 'Oh, I'm only a farmer! If that's your opinion, then I'll—'

The affair would end then, I hoped. She would never see him again. The 'business' between Marian and Ted had spoilt my holiday. It had spoilt Marian's visit to London. It was pushing Ted away from the things he loved. It was urging him to do something that he would hate. Other things seemed small and unimportant. It filled our minds, and all our actions depended on it.

At that time I did not know the word *passion*. I did not understand the power that drew them together. It gave them something that I did not get. I was jealous of the thing that it gave them. Or jealous of the thing that they gave each other. My experience could not tell me anything about passion. But I was beginning to guess something about it.

I decided to make a spell which would break Ted's spell on Marian. My spell would not harm either of them, but it would destroy Ted's spell. My spell would have a better chance of success if it was a difficult one. I had to frighten myself while I was making it. I should have to do something that I feared. The right idea came to me while I was talking to Marcus. But I do not think he noticed any change in my conversation.

Marcus and I went to bed at our usual time. Half an hour later I put on some clothes and crept down the stairs. I stopped outside the door of the main room. Inside, Marian was playing the piano, and someone was singing. The front door of the house was open. It was open every night in order to keep the house cool. But it was not cool, and I was sweating.

I was frightened of the thing I had planned. The song ended, and I almost knocked at the door. I could say to Mrs Maudsley: 'I'm still awake. Can I listen to the music?' I looked towards the darkness outside. I did not think that I was brave enough to go out there.

The voices inside were discussing the next song. I crept to the door again and must have touched it with my foot. I heard Mrs Maudsley's voice.

'Denys, I think I heard a noise outside the door. Please see if anyone is there.'

Denys's steps came towards the door, and I ran outside into the darkness.

One of my fears was that I should lose my way in the darkness. Another was that the front door would be shut and locked before I returned. Then I should have to stay outside and try to sleep on the ground. But it was not completely dark, and I soon found the path.

My spell had to be made at night. I was sure that darkness would give it extra strength. I ran alone between the bushes. As I went, I reminded myself of the details of my plan.

Every part of the deadly nightshade was a strong poison. So the spell would have more effect if every part of the plant was used. I needed leaf, stem, flower, fruit and root. I had brought a knife in order to cut off part of the root. While I was gathering these things, no part of the plant should touch my lips. I would then carry everything back to my room.

In my room the necessary things were ready. They were:

> Four candles (to heat the liquid)
> One silver cup.
> One soap dish (with holes in it)
> Four small books (to support the soap dish)
> Four boxes of matches
> Water
> Watch (to measure the exact time)
> Wet cloth (to guard against fire)

My mother had given me the silver cup. She had thought that I might need it for tea-parties in the park. The metal was very thin, so it would be easy to heat the liquid.

The success of my spell depended on the soap dish. It would be supported on two opposite sides by the books. The candles would burn between the books. I intended to place the cup in the soap dish. The candle flames would pass through the holes in the soap dish and heat the cup.

The cup would contain a little water and pieces of the plant. It should boil at twelve o'clock exactly. At the same time I would repeat the words of the spell thirteen times. Then I would say, 'And I am thirteen, too.' If I sweated, some drops of sweat should be added to the liquid. Later, I intended to get rid of the liquid in the bathroom.

I had written all these details in my diary. After the experiment, I planned to tear the pages out. But I forgot to do that. The next day,

I would repeat the words of the spell thirteen times.

Friday, I forgot many other things, too.

My eyes got used to the darkness. I reached the huts and saw the deadly nightshade. It was like a lady at the door of her house. 'Come in,' it seemed to say. I thought that it wanted me. I needed it in order to make my spell. But I felt sure now that the deadly nightshade needed me more. It wanted to make a spell itself.

I stretched out my hand and touched the flowers and leaves. They held my hand. If I went inside the hut, I should learn its secret. And it would learn mine. I went in. It was hot and soft and comfortable inside. A flower touched my face. Some of the fruit rubbed against my lips . . .

When that happened, I was very frightened. I turned and tried to go out. But I could not find the way. There seemed to be a wall on every side. I was so frightened now that I began to break the plant. I made a clear space round my head, but that was not enough. The plant was not as strong as I had feared. I fought with it. I broke its main stem. Leaves, flowers and fruit fell to the ground round me. I seized the stem and pulled with all my strength. The roots began to crack in the ground. The plant struggled to defend itself. And then it gave up the fight. The roots came out of the ground, and I fell on my back outside. The deadly nightshade was destroyed.

Chapter 22

I slept very well that night. I did not wake up until a servant came into my room.

'Good morning, Henry!' I said.

'Good morning, sir,' he answered. 'I hope you will have a happy birthday.'

'Of course, it's my birthday!' I cried. 'I had forgotten it.'

'The others haven't forgotten,' he said.

Something in the room seemed different, and something inside me felt strange. I looked at the window.

'Is it raining?' I asked. The colour of the sky was quite a surprise to me.

'Not yet,' he replied. 'But I'm sure it will rain today. The ground needs some water. All this hot weather isn't natural.'

'Oh, but it's summer!' I exclaimed.

'It isn't natural,' Henry repeated. 'Everything is burnt brown. And a lot of people have gone mad.'

'Gone mad?' I said. 'Do you mean that the heat has made them go mad?' I was very interested in madness.

'Yes,' he said. 'It isn't only dogs that go mad. People do, too.'

'Do you know anybody who has gone mad?' I asked.

'I don't want to say anything about that,' he replied. 'But I may know somebody who has.'

For a moment I thought about the strange passion of Marian and Ted. And I wondered whether that was caused by the heat.

Henry had brought some hot water into the room, and he poured it into the bowl.

'The soap dish has gone,' he said.

'It's there,' I said, and pointed to the table.

He walked across and examined the things on the table. The little pile looked like some ancient sacrifice. The four candles were between the four books. The soap dish rested on the books. My silver cup was in the soap dish. There were the four boxes of matches and the wet cloth.

Henry shook his head slowly. I guessed his thoughts: this boy has also gone mad in the heat.

'You've been enjoying yourself, haven't you?' he said.

As soon as he had gone, I put everything in its proper place. In the light of day the things did not seem at all evil. They had even seemed harmless after my struggle with the deadly nightshade. Everything had been easy after that battle. The front door was still open when I had come back to the house. And I had been afraid of nothing.

Now the sky was grey. That was one reason why I felt strange. The sun seemed to have gone, and it was like the loss of a dear friend. I was so used to the heat that I hated this change. And there was another change. When I had destroyed the deadly nightshade, some of my old ideas had suffered, too. I seemed to understand, quite suddenly, that my spells were rather foolish. It was my thirteenth birthday, and perhaps I was too old now to believe in spells and magic. I must learn how to control my imagination.

It had all started when Jenkins and Strode had fallen off the roof. But my curses had not *caused* the accident. I now believed that it might have happened to anyone. And the fever at school was the same: the boys would have got it even if I had not written a spell. I was just pretending to have some special power, and this pretence had deceived a lot of boys. It had also deceived myself, and that was even worse. I blamed my imagination for most of the trouble.

At Brandham I had pretended that I could control the weather. I thought I could stop the affair between Marian and Ted. Marian had made me feel that she was depending on me. So my foolish ideas were partly her fault. I felt ashamed of them now and ashamed, too, of my attempts to influence the events of life.

Perhaps Henry was right: my struggle with the deadly nightshade might have been one of the effects of the heat. The heat might have made my brain soft, and a part of it had gone mad. The heat and Marian had made Mrs Maudsley ill. Perhaps it was also the cause of Marcus's fever. But he had not *pretended* anything. He never deceived himself. He was interested in the things that actually happened. He never tried to change them or to imagine other events. That was why he could not keep a secret. He would rather tell the secret and then wait for something to happen. When I thought about these things, I admired Marcus very much.

What would he have said if he had seen my attack on the deadly nightshade? What would anyone have said? He would have thought that I was mad. And everyone would have agreed. I was almost ready to agree myself.

Henry had put my green suit and other clothes on a chair, but I decided not to wear it. The colour did not worry me at all now, but the suit reminded me of my pretence. So I put on my thick suit, stockings and heavy boots.

At breakfast I received congratulations on my birthday. Some of the guests made a few jokes about my suit. I did not imagine any insults, and so their remarks did not worry me. Two weeks ago the same jokes had made me cry!

Lord Trimingham said, 'Leo is quite right. It's going to rain today. We shall all have to change our clothes, but he won't.'

I noticed then that everyone was wearing thin summer clothes.

Marian said, 'Yes. That suit would be right for a journey by train. I hope you're not going away, Leo.'

Beside my plate there were two long envelopes, and I recognized the writing. They were from my mother and my aunt. I usually read my letters in my room, but today I wanted all my actions to be public. So I asked everyone to excuse me, and I opened my mother's letter.

She seemed sorry that she had not sent me the telegram. She hoped that I was happy again. 'If you are still taking the messages,' she wrote, 'ask Mrs Maudsley to give them to a servant. I'm sure she would. I hope this small present will match your new suit.'

I looked into the envelope and took out—a long green tie.

'Oh, that *is* a lovely tie!' several voices exclaimed.

'But it doesn't match the suit you're wearing,' Marian said.

The other letter was longer because my aunt always wrote a lot about herself. She also liked to guess what I was doing. And her guesses were usually quite good ones.

'Your mother told me that you have a new suit,' she wrote. 'Green is an unusual colour for a boy's suit, perhaps, but I like it. *I think men's clothes are always too dull, don't you?* People say that a woman can never choose a man's tie. But I think that's nonsense. I've chosen this one for you!'

It was a bow-tie. The colour was almost yellow, and I did not like it very much. The bow was already tied in a beautiful knot, so it would be very easy to put on.

But my friends did not seem to approve of it, and doubts spread through the room. I guessed that Marcus was quite ready to criticize it. Suddenly Lord Trimingham stretched out his hand and said:

'Can I have a look at it, Leo?'

He took off his own blue and white bow-tie and put on mine. 'I think it's very gay,' he said. 'It's the right kind of tie for Goodwood Races.'

I kept that tie for many years.

'*Today* is Leo's day,' Mrs Maudsley said, after breakfast. 'What would you like to do, Leo?'

I could not think of an answer, so Mrs Maudsley tried to help me.

'Shall we have a drive into the country and take lunch with us?'

'That would be very nice,' I said.

'Or would you like to visit Beeston Castle after lunch? You haven't seen it, have you?'

'That would be very nice,' I repeated, miserably.

'So if it doesn't rain, we'll go to Beeston Castle,' she said. 'You can play with Marcus all the morning. And at five o'clock you'll cut your birthday cake.'

'But Mother,' Denys said, 'we still don't know what *Leo* wants.'

'I think we do,' Mrs Maudsley said calmly. 'You agree, Leo, don't you?'

'Oh, *yes*,' I said.

Mrs Maudsley turned to her elder son. 'Are you satisfied, Denys?'

'We ought to let Leo choose on his birthday,' Denys said.

'But hasn't he chosen?' his mother asked.

'No, Mother, you've chosen for him.'

Mrs Maudsley's face expressed a prayer for patience.

'Leo did not suggest anything,' she said, 'so—'

'I know, Mother, but on his *birthday*—'

'Can you suggest anything, Denys?' she asked.

'No, Mother, it isn't *my* birthday.'

Mrs Maudsley looked angry. 'That's enough,' she said. 'Leo has agreed to the arrangements.'

Outside, Marcus said to me: 'No, Leo, you can't wear that tie.'

'Why not?'

'Because the bow is already tied. Trimingham could wear it, of course. He can wear anything, but you have to dress with care.'

'Why?' I asked.

'You mustn't look common,' he replied. 'But I won't say any more because it's your birthday.'

During the morning I tried not to use my imagination. And I soon noticed that the morning was not very exciting. It was my birthday, but the birthday spirit seemed to be absent. The day was not much different from any other day. I was afraid to visit the hut where I had killed the deadly nightshade. (I knew that a murderer likes to go back to the scene of his crime.) If I went there, I should certainly imagine all kinds of things. I did not feel happy even with Marcus, although he was being specially kind to me.

I did not want to change my present opinion of spells and curses. They were useless, even foolish, and I was too old to believe in them. But by lunch-time I knew that I could hardly treat my imagination in the same way. It was a part of my character. I had had it all my life. It provided me with some of the pleasures that I most enjoyed. I tried very hard to imitate Marcus's habit of telling me all his thoughts. But I could not do it. I knew secrets that were too dangerous to talk about. I tried to think only about the events that actually happened. But I soon knew that there was very little pleasure in that. I felt uncomfortable in my thick suit, and my spirit felt uncomfortable without my imagination. I almost wished that Marcus would quarrel with me. When that idea crept into my mind, I had to change my plan. I knew that I should never be happy without my own private thoughts.

I went to my room then and put on my green suit. After that I felt a lot better.

Chapter 23

After lunch the sky was dark with clouds, and we all expected thunder. Mrs Maudsley decided to wait for a quarter of an hour. If then there was still the threat of thunder, we would not go to Beeston Castle.

We were all standing near the front door. Marian said, 'Come with me, Leo, and tell me about the weather.'

I followed her outside and looked up at the sky. 'I think—' I began.

'You needn't,' she said. 'If we don't go to Beeston, would you like a walk?'

'Oh, yes,' I said eagerly. 'Will you come with me?'

'I'd like to,' she answered, 'but it's not that kind of walk. It's this.' As she was speaking her hand touched mine. She gave me a letter.

'Oh no!' I cried. I felt disappointed and angry.

'But I say "Yes".' She was not annoyed with me this time, but she began to laugh loudly. She was laughing, I thought, so as to hide my surprise and disappointment from the others. Perhaps she wanted them to think that we were having a joke. But it was not a joke, and I started arguing with her. That made her laugh more, and then, in despair, I laughed too. I laughed louder than she did. We must have made a lot of noise. She had not expected me to laugh with her, I thought.

'Marian! Leo!'

It was Mrs Maudsley's voice. She walked slowly down the steps. Marian was still laughing, but I had stopped.

'What are you arguing about?' Mrs Maudsley asked.

'Oh, I was teaching him some good manners,' Marian said. She did not say any more because at that moment I dropped the letter. It lay on the ground between us.

'Were you arguing about that letter?' Mrs Maudsley asked.

Marian picked it up and pushed it into my pocket.

'Yes, Mother,' she said. 'I asked Leo to take it to Nannie Robson. I'd like to visit her this afternoon. But Leo refused to take it! He pretended that he and Marcus were busy.'

'It needn't worry you, Marian,' Mrs Maudsley said. She looked directly at Marian and then at me. 'You say that she never remembers your visits. I thought that Leo and I might have a walk in the garden. It isn't fine enough to go to Beeston this afternoon. Come, Leo. You haven't yet seen the garden properly. Marcus doesn't like flowers very much.'

It was true that I had not seen the garden properly. I preferred the rubbish heap, where I hoped to find something of value. But I liked flowers, especially those that trapped insects. They could catch insects and change them into a kind of soup. But I had an idea that I needed some protection from Mrs Maudsley. So I said:

'Would you like Marcus to come with us?'

'Oh, no,' she said. 'You've been playing with him all the morning. He's very fond of you, Leo, and Marian is, too. We all are.'

I was delighted with this speech but did not know the proper

'Come, Leo. You haven't yet seen the garden properly.'

answer. I tried to imagine the answer that my mother would give.

'You have all been very kind to me,' I said.

'Have we? I thought we might have neglected you. First Marcus was ill, and then I was in bed for a few days. I hope the others looked after you.'

'Oh, yes, they did,' I said.

We had reached the garden.

'Are you really interested in flowers?' she asked.

I said that I was very interested in dangerous flowers.

She smiled. 'There aren't many of that kind here.'

I told her about the deadly nightshade.

'It was in one of those old huts,' I said, 'behind the house.'

I stopped then. I did not want to go on.

Marcus and I had heard the voices near those huts. I wondered whether he had told his mother about them. 'Do you often go along that path?' she asked. 'Aren't you frightened of the darkness in those old ruins?'

'There might be thieves there,' I said.

'Do you mean real thieves?'

'No, but I like to pretend.'

We stopped by a big pink flower, and Mrs Maudsley said:

'This always reminds me of Marian. Do you often carry messages for her?'

I thought as quickly as I could.

'No, not often,' I said. 'Just once or twice.'

'I'm worried because of that note to Nannie Robson. Would you like to go now? You know the way, of course.'

This was an opportunity. I could escape if I wished. But what should I say to her?

'I'd like to go. I'm not quite sure of the way, but I can ask someone.'

'Ask someone?' she repeated. 'But haven't you taken messages there before?'

'Oh, yes. Yes, I have.'

'Why aren't you sure of the way then?'

I did not answer.

'Listen,' she said. 'Someone should deliver that note. You have it in your pocket, haven't you? I'll call one of the servants and ask him to take it.'

I felt a cold sweat on my skin. 'Oh no, Mrs Maudsley,' I said. 'It isn't very important.'

'It's important to Nannie Robson,' Mrs Maudsley said. 'Old people like to prepare something for a visitor.'

Then she called one of the men who were working there. He put down his tools and came towards us. I thought he had a cruel face. I put my hand in my pocket.

The man took off his cap.

'Stanton,' Mrs Maudsley said, 'we have a rather urgent note for Miss Robson. Would you mind taking it?'

Stanton agreed and held out his hand.

My fingers moved in my pocket. I felt in several of them and then said: 'I haven't got it! I'm very sorry. It must have fallen out somewhere.'

'Feel again,' Mrs Maudsley said. 'Feel again.'

I felt in all my pockets but did not take out the note.

Mrs Maudsley said, 'Stanton, just tell Miss Robson that Miss Marian will visit her this afternoon.'

I wanted to follow Stanton when he left us. But I could not do that. Mrs Maudsley was looking at me steadily.

She said, 'Take your hands out of your pockets, please. You shouldn't stand like that. It's bad manners.'

'I haven't got it! I'm very sorry.'

I obeyed but did not speak.

'I could search your pockets,' she said, 'but I won't do that. You said that you have taken messages for Marian before. I want to ask you one question. If you don't take them to Nannie Robson, to whom do you take them?'

I could not answer. But an answer came from the sky. There was a crash of thunder. Rain began immediately. We ran to the house. And when we reached it, I went straight to my room. There, I received another shock. All my things had gone. Some other guest must have arrived and was using the room. I stayed in the bathroom until tea-time. Everything was ready for my birthday tea. The cake was in the middle of the table. The pink candles were lit in a circle around it.

'Sit beside me, please, Leo,' Mrs Maudsley said.

I crept to that uncomfortable place, but I need not have worried. Her manner had changed.

'I'm sorry about your room,' she said. 'We needed it for another guest. Your things are in Marcus's room. Are you pleased to share with him again?'

'Yes, of course,' I said.

'Marian wants to give you her present first,' she said. 'Don't try to guess what it is. The other presents are on that table there.' And she pointed across the room.

There were several parcels on the table. I tried to guess what might be in them. The shapes of the parcels did not help me much.

'Can you wait?' Mrs Maudsley asked.

'When is Marian coming?'

'About six o'clock, we think. She won't stay very long with Nannie Robson.'

She smiled. But I noticed that her hands were shaking.

'Did you get wet?' I asked. I had to refer to our talk in some way. I could not believe that she had forgotten it.

'Not very wet.' She laughed. 'But if you'd been a gentleman, you'd have waited for me.'

'But he *is* a gentleman,' Lord Trimingham said. 'He's quite a lady-killer. Marian has great faith in him.'

Mrs Maudsley changed the subject. She said, 'It's time that Leo blew out the candles and cut the cake.'

Someone put the cake in front of me. I took a big breath and blew. The other guests blew too, and soon all the candles were out. I cut a few pieces of the cake.

Lord Trimingham looked at his watch. 'Marian ought to be here now,' he said.

'It's still raining,' Mr Maudsley said. 'We'd better send a carriage to Nannie Robson's house. Why didn't we think of that before?' He rang the bell and gave the order.

'Was it raining when she went out?' somebody asked. But no one could answer. No one had seen her going.

'You have a very kind daughter, Mrs Maudsley,' another guest said. 'Not many girls have patience with their old nurses.'

We ate the cake, but left one thick piece on the plate for Marian. The carriage drove past the windows.

'She'll be here in ten minutes,' Lord Trimingham said.

'She may not have waited for the carriage,' someone said. 'She may be walking in the rain. She'll be so wet that she'll have to change her clothes.'

Mrs Maudsley gave everyone another cup of tea, and there was a pause in the conversation. For the last fifteen minutes there had been a pause after every action and almost every remark. At one time everybody seemed to be talking. And it was then that I heard the noise of the carriage outside. A few minutes later the butler came into the room and spoke to Mrs Maudsley.

'Excuse me,' he said. 'The carriage has come back but not Miss Marian. She wasn't at Miss Robson's. Miss Robson said that she hadn't seen her today.'

Although I had been expecting this news, it still gave me a shock. I felt very miserable.

'Where *can* she be?' someone asked.

'Yes, where can she be?'

'She may be in her room,' Denys said. 'Perhaps she's changing her clothes.'

'We shall just have to wait for her,' Mr Maudsley said, calmly.

But Mrs Maudsley pushed her chair back and stood up. Her body was bent and trembling. I could hardly recognize her face.

'No,' she said. 'We won't wait. I'm going to look for her. Leo, you know where she is. You shall show me the way.'

I hardly knew what was happening. She caught my hand and pulled me behind her. 'Madeleine!' her husband cried. It was the only time that I ever heard her name.

Outside the room I saw the green bicycle, and I have never forgotten that first quick look at it. It was resting against the post of the staircase and shining as brightly as silver.

Then we were outside in the rain. I did not know that Mrs Maudsley could run fast. She ran so fast now that I could hardly stay beside her. We were soon very wet, but I was too frightened to worry about the rain.

Mrs Maudsley said nothing. She ran with wide, awkward steps, and her skirt was dragging through the mud. It was soon clear that she was guiding me. She knew where we were going. When we came to the path between the bushes, I tried to turn her back.

I cried, 'Not this way, Mrs Maudsley!'

She did not listen to me but hurried forward. Then we reached the hut where I had killed the deadly nightshade. The broken roots and branches were still lying on the path. She stopped and looked inside the hut.

'Not here,' she said, moving away, 'but here, perhaps . . . or here.'

There was no sound from the row of huts. I did not want to search with her, and I tried to free my hand from hers. I began to cry.

'No,' she said, 'you *must* come with me.' And she pulled me forward.

And then we saw them. They were lying together on the ground. Marian and Ted Burgess. I did not understand. But I guessed that

It was soon clear that she was guiding me. She knew where we were going.

they were spooning. Mrs Maudsley's loud cries frightened me. They were louder than any cries that I had ever heard.

I remember very little more. I must have been ill, because I stayed in bed for two or three days. But before I left Brandham Hall, I heard and understood one thing: Ted Burgess had gone home that evening and shot himself.

Epilogue

My illness lasted about six weeks, and I do not remember very much about it. Someone must have brought me home to West Hatch. The doctor and my mother tried to make me remember the last events at Brandham. But I would not have said anything even if I had been able to remember.

'You haven't done anything *bad*, Leo,' my mother used to say. 'You needn't feel ashamed. Besides, it's all over now.'

But I did not believe her. I felt ashamed of many things. And I did not believe that it was all over. I thought that I had made them all suffer—Lord Trimingham, Ted, Marian and all the Maudsley family. I did not know, and did not want to know, the results of my actions. Doubtless, they were as serious as Mrs Maudsley's cries had been.

For Ted Burgess the result was death. That was partly why my experience at Brandham was not 'all over'. In my mind there were the most terrible pictures of Ted's dead body. And there was always a picture of him cleaning his gun. He had cleaned it, I imagined, in order to shoot himself with it. But I knew that was not true. He might have had many thoughts while he was cleaning his gun. But the idea of shooting himself must have been furthest from his mind.

I did not consider the idea that the people at Brandham had treated me badly. I did not really know how to blame a grown-up person. There had been a set of facts which I had to deal with. I had succeeded in the cricket match and at the concert, but in the third test I had failed. When Mrs Maudsley had discovered Marian and Ted together on the ground, she had defeated me. And now I was *vanquished* for ever.

At school my spells had brought me victory, and at Brandham, too, my last spell had been a success. At least, it had stopped the affair between Ted and Marian. It had also destroyed the deadly nightshade. But then, like some dangerous pet, it had turned against its master. It had destroyed Ted and perhaps destroyed me.

I had come into Ted's life by chance. A strange boy from some distant place had appeared and slid down the straw stack at Black Farm. From that moment, I now believed, Ted's fate was certain. And mine was certain too, because our fates were joined together. I could not harm him without harming myself.

At school I had used my magic power to influence ordinary people and ordinary events. At Brandham I had tried to use it against people who were *not* ordinary. And that was why it had failed. I had tried to make the gods fight one another!

My experience at Brandham seemed to kill my faith in other people and most of my love for them. It also proved that my imagination had been a kind of trap. From then until now I have lived mainly without friends. I have enjoyed little love and little of the happiness that love brings. I have managed to live without the great pleasure that my imagination used to provide.

When Marcus and I met again at school, we were polite but not friendly. No one noticed this because the other boys there often changed their friends. I did not tell anyone about my holiday at Brandham. And gradually the names Brandham, Maudsley and Trimingham lost their power to frighten me. Indeed, as time passed, I became less and less interested in people in almost every way. Another pleasure came to my aid: the pleasure that I had always gained from facts. I began to collect facts, and I soon recognized their great value. They were independent of me, and my private wishes could not change them. I thought they were the only true things in the world. My facts had no love in them and certainly no passion. They did not add much to my experience of life or to my imagination, but they served me instead of both. Ted Burgess had been afraid to tell me the facts of life, but that did not worry me now. I preferred the life of facts! They served me well, too, and probably saved my life.

The First Great War started in 1914. I was twenty-seven then, but I did not have to join the army. The government thought that my skill with facts was more important work.

My mother had kept all the letters that I had written to her. They were not in the red box where I had found the diary. But I soon discovered them and decided to read them again. They might help, I thought, to explain some of the problems of my Brandham experience.

One thing became clear immediately. Marian had been quite fond of me *before* the messages started. She had later increased her favours and told me a lot of lies. But the green suit came first. I understood now the chief reason for our visit to Norwich: she wanted to meet Ted Burgess. He was the man who had raised his hat to her. But she was also worried about the heat and my thick woollen suit.

It was certain, too, that Marcus always told his mother everything. He had made me so angry once that I boasted about Marian. I claimed to know where she went in the evenings. And he must have repeated the claim to his mother. My stupid boasting had been the real cause of all the trouble. At school Marcus knew how to keep a secret, but at home he behaved differently. I did not know then that people's habits changed according to their situations.

For several months after my visit to Brandham, I blamed myself for everything that had happened there. I thought that I should not have read Marian's note to Ted. I should not have changed the time in Ted's last message to her. If I had told her 'half past six', my birthday party would have been a great success. Mrs Maudsley would not then have gone out to look for Marian. My intention had been good, but the result had been very bad. Since that time I have never interfered, for good or bad, in other people's business.

When, later, I considered my spells, especially the last one, I had to shake my head. They were absolute nonsense, of course. They did not agree at all with the world of facts. In time it was the search for facts that brought peace to my mind.

My memory and my diary provided enough facts for this story. But the facts did not satisfy me. Like the brass plates on the wall of Brandham Church, they were not complete. They did not tell me whether my decisions were wise. I did not know whether I had failed in life or whether I had succeeded. They told me nothing about happiness or unhappiness. I needed other facts with which I could compare my own. And I should have to get them from *other* people—the other people in the story. That was the trouble now. Their names did not worry me, but I did not want to meet them.

Marian, Mrs Maudsley, Trimingham, Marcus: I thought of them all as figures in a picture. They did not seem to exist at present. Brandham Hall and the year 1900 formed the strong frame of the picture. I did not think that they could ever move outside that frame.

But at that moment my thoughts were interrupted. I discovered a letter. There was no address on the envelope, and it had never been opened. I remembered it immediately. It was Marian's last note to Ted. My mother must have found it in my pocket when I had come home. Mrs Maudsley had almost found it, too. If she *had* found it, everything would have been different! But I was interested only in facts, and the note might contain a new one. I opened the envelope and read:

Darling,

Our trusted messenger must have made a mistake. You *can't*
have said six o'clock. At that time there'll be straw in your hair
and dust on your clothes! I can hardly meet you in that condition.
So come at half past six if you can. It's our dear messenger's
birthday, and I must be there to give him a present. It's exactly
the right present for a messenger. He won't have to walk to the
farm in future! I'm giving him this note. Mother is making other
plans for him. Although he is very clever, Mother may be cleverer!
If he doesn't deliver it, I shall be there at six. And I'll wait till
seven or eight or nine—darling, darling.

Tears came into my eyes. They were my first tears for more than
fifty years. She had given me the bicycle for my journeys to the
farm! I wished now that I had kept it. After my illness I had told
my mother to give it away. I had never ridden it.

The figures in the picture started to move. I wanted to know what
had happened to them all. And I decided to go back to Brandham.

I stayed at the hotel in Norwich where Marian and I had had
lunch. The next day I hired a car and drove to the village.

The place had changed of course and, after fifty years, I did not
recognize it. I wondered where I might find the least change. And I
knew that that would be the church. I went there immediately.

There were two new brass plates on the wall.

'Hugh Winlove, ninth Viscount Trimingham,' I read. 'Born
November 15th 1874, died July 6th 1910.'

Poor Hugh! He had lived for only ten years after my visit. A
doctor would not have been surprised, I thought. He had once
seemed a much older person than I. But now I imagined a much
younger man. He had died when he was thirty-six. I wondered
whether he had died from the effects of his wound.

I wondered, too, whether he had ever married. The plate did not
mention a Viscountess, but I turned to the other new one. It was far
from the others in the corner of the wall.

'Hugh Maudsley Winlove, tenth Viscount Trimingham. Born
February 12th 1901, killed in the Battle of Normandy, June 15th
1944. And Alethea, his wife, killed in an air attack on London,
January 16th 1941.'

If these were facts, then I did not understand them. Lord
Trimingham was not married when I left Brandham Hall. But this
plate showed that he had had a son six or seven months later. It was

very strange.

I know now why I did not guess the truth. I had always supposed that Marian would have died. In my thoughts she had died immediately after that last terrible scene at the huts. I did not think that she could ever go on living. And even after fifty years that idea was still firmly in my mind.

I looked for a plate in memory of the eleventh Viscount, but I could not find one. Unless he was still alive, then the family had ended.

I left the church and walked down the main street of the village. My plan was a simple one. I hoped to find the oldest person there. He or she would be able to tell me the necessary facts. I noticed several people in shops or in their gardens. And then I saw a man whose face seemed less unfamiliar than the others. He was about twenty-five years old and not the kind of person I was looking for. But there was one question that he might be able to answer.

'Excuse me,' I said, 'but is there still a Lord Trimingham at Brandham Hall?'

At first I thought that he did not want to answer. He seemed annoyed that I had interrupted his thoughts.

He said, 'There is, and in fact I am Lord Trimingham.'

I was very surprised and looked hard at his face. It was the colour of his skin that reminded me of something. It was the colour of ripe corn.

'You seem surprised,' he said. 'I live only in a corner of the house. The rest of it has become a school for girls.'

'I'm sorry,' I said. 'But I'm glad you live there. I stayed there many years ago.'

His manner changed immediately, and he said, almost eagerly:

'Did you really? Then you must know the house.'

'I remember parts of it,' I said.

'When did you stay there?'

'It was when your grandfather was alive,' I said.

'My grandfather?' he said. And I noticed that his manner changed again. He seemed anxious about something. 'Did you know my grandfather?'

'Yes,' I said, 'the ninth Viscount. He was your grandfather, wasn't he?'

'Of course,' Lord Trimingham said, 'of course. I never knew him, I'm afraid. He died before I was born. But I've heard about him. I believe he was a very nice man.'

I smiled. 'He was, indeed,' I said.

'And did you also know my grandmother?'

I was surprised once again, and wanted time to think.

'Your grandmother?' I said.

'Yes, she was a Miss Maudsley,' he said.

I took a long breath. 'Oh yes,' I said. 'I knew her very well. Is she still alive?'

'She is,' he said. But there was not much gladness in his voice.

'And where does she live?'

'Here, in the village. She lives in a little house that used to belong to Miss Robson. Did you know her, too?'

'No,' I said. 'I never saw her, but I heard about her. — Is your grandmother well?'

'Quite well,' he said, 'but she forgets things rather easily. Many old people do, of course.' He smiled then, and went on: 'Why don't you go and see her? I'm sure she'd like to see you. She's rather lonely. She doesn't have many visitors.'

The past seemed to rise in front of me and take control of my voice. 'I'd better not,' I said. 'She may not want to see me.'

He was puzzled, I knew. He said, 'You must decide about that.'

He was a much younger man than I. And that, I thought, might give me a claim to his assistance. I decided to speak freely.

'Will you be kind enough to help me?' I asked.

'Of course. But how?'

'Will you tell Lady Trimingham that Leo Colston is here. Say that I would like to see her.'

'Leo Colston?' he repeated.

'Yes, that is my name.'

He hesitated. 'I don't usually go to her house,' he said. 'I telephone sometimes. — Was there a telephone here when you came before?'

'No,' I replied. 'It would have helped a lot if there had been.'

'Yes, indeed,' he said. 'My grandmother talks a lot. But I'll go if you like. — I—' He stopped then.

'I'd be very glad if you did,' I said firmly. 'I don't want to—to surprise her.' I thought of the last time I had done so.

'I'll go,' he said. 'It's Mr Leo Colston, isn't it? Do you think she'll remember the name?'

'I'm sure she will,' I said. 'I'll wait here for you.'

While I was waiting I wandered about the street. But I saw nothing that I could remember. I even stood outside the village hall. I ought to have remembered the red-brick building because it was the scene of my last public success. But I did not.

Then I saw the young man and went to meet him. His face looked worried, and it reminded me very strongly of Ted Burgess.

'She didn't remember you at first,' he said. 'And then she remembered you very well. She said she would be very pleased to see you. She was worried about lunch. She asked me to give it to you because she can't. Would you like that?'

'Yes,' I replied, 'if it's no trouble.'

'I would be happy if you came,' he said. But he did not look at all happy. 'Grandmother wasn't sure that you'd want to come to the Hall.'

'Oh, why?' I asked.

'Because of something that happened long ago. You were only a little boy, she said. And she said it wasn't her fault.'

'Your grandfather used to say that nothing is ever a lady's fault,' I said.

He looked very hard at me.

'Yes,' I said, 'I knew your grandfather very well indeed, and you are very like him.'

He changed colour. And I noticed that he was standing away from me. His real grandfather had stood just like that when we last met.

His face was red now. 'I'm very sorry,' he said, 'if we didn't treat you well.'

I liked his saying 'we'. And I remembered how sorry Ted had been about many things. I said quickly:

'Oh, it happened long, long ago. Please don't think about it. Your grandmother—'

'Yes?' he said.

'Do you often see her?'

'Not very often.'

'And not many people visit her. Is that right?'

'Not very many,' he said.

'Did many people visit her when she lived at the Hall?'

He shook his head. 'I don't think so.'

'Then why does she go on living in the village?'

'I just don't know,' he said.

'She was very beautiful.'

'I've often heard that,' he said. 'But I don't quite see it. — Do you know the way to the house?'

'No, but I can ask someone.' I remembered that I had given the same answer once before. To Mrs Maudsley.

He did not offer to go with me, but he showed me the way. Then he added: 'We'll have lunch about one o'clock.' And I promised to be there. He walked away, but after a moment he turned. He came back and then stopped. Without looking at me, he said:

'Were you the little boy who—?'

'Yes,' I said.

Marian was sitting in front of a window. When I entered the room, a young woman servant said, 'Mr Colston'. Marian got up and held out her hand uncertainly.

'Is this really—?' she began.

'I would have known you,' I said. 'But I didn't expect you would know me.'

Actually, if I had seen her in the street, I would not have recognized her. There was a slight blueness in the colour of her hair, and she did not now have a round face. Her nose seemed larger. She used a lot of powder and other colour on her face and lips. Only her eyes had kept their quality, although they had faded.

We talked a little about my journey, and I told her something of my work. Then I said:

'I don't suppose my life has been a very exciting one.'

This was true. Nothing unusual had happened to me since I had lost my memory at Brandham Hall.

She said, 'You lost your memory at the beginning of your life. I'm losing mine at the end. It isn't serious, of course. But sometimes I'm not quite sure what happened yesterday. Nannie Robson used to be like that. I remember the past very clearly.'

I asked her several questions then, and she said:

'Marcus was killed in the first war, and Denys, too. I think Denys was killed first. Marcus was your friend, wasn't he? Yes, of course he was. A boy with a round face: he was Mother's favourite, and mine too.'

'What happened to your mother?' I asked.

'Poor Mother! It was very sad. But I was soon well again. We didn't have the ball, of course. Your mother came here, and I remember her well. She was a sweet woman, with grey eyes, like yours, and brown hair. But the Hall was full, and so we arranged a room for her in the village. You didn't speak to anyone for two or three days, and Mother wouldn't stop crying. It was a terrible time! Then suddenly Father began to give orders. By the next day everyone who could travel had gone. You stayed until Monday, I remember. We never found out how you had heard about Ted. Perhaps Henry told you. Wasn't he one of your friends?'

'How did you know that I had heard?'

'Because you said just two things. You said, 'Why did Ted shoot himself? I thought he could shoot straight.' You must have thought it was an accident. But it wasn't, of course. Ted had a weak spot in his character, like Edward.'

'Edward?'

'My grandson. Ted needn't have killed himself. People soon forget that kind of thing. They would forget it as soon as I became Lady Trimingham.'

'And Hugh?' I asked.

'He married me. He didn't worry about it. Hugh was as true as steel. He wouldn't listen to a word of criticism. If people didn't want to know us, we didn't think about them. But we had lots of friends. I was Lady Trimingham, of course. I still am. There isn't another.'

'What was your son's wife like?' I asked.

'Poor Alethea? Oh, she was a very miserable girl. And her parties were such miserable affairs that I hardly ever went to them. But people came to me, of course—interesting people, like artists and writers. My son wasn't fond of living in the country. He was like my father, but he hadn't Father's strong character. Father was a wonderful man, and Mother was wonderful, too. I was lucky to have parents like them.'

'You haven't told me about your mother,' I reminded her.

'Poor Mother! She couldn't stay with us, of course. She had to go to hospital, but we often went to see her. She was glad that I married Hugh.'

'And your father?'

'Oh, Father lived until he was nearly ninety. But he retired when Marcus and Denys were killed. He often came to see us at the Hall. And he visited me for many years after Hugh died. We were all very fond of one another.'

My life, I thought, had been very happy. And hers had been unhappy. I did not want to hear much more, but the facts were not yet complete.

'Aren't you lonely here, Marian?' I asked. 'Wouldn't you be happier in London?'

'Lonely?' she said. 'What do you mean? Lots of people come to see me. They all know about me. They know what happened here. And, naturally, they want to see me—just as you did.'

'I'm very glad I came. And I was pleased to meet your grandson, Edward.'

'You mustn't call him Edward,' she said. 'It's a family name, of course, but he prefers Hugh.'

'You must be very glad that he's near you,' I said.

Her manner changed then, and her face changed, too. I thought that she might be going to cry.

'I am,' she said. Then she corrected herself: 'I would be if he came to see me. Although we are the only two in the family now, he doesn't come often.'

'Doesn't he?' I said.

'No. Hundreds of other people come, but he doesn't; at least, not regularly. Do you remember how often I used to visit old Nannie Robson?'

Before I could say anything, she asked: 'Does he remind you of anyone?'

I was surprised that she asked me that question. 'Yes, he does,' I said. 'His grandfather.'

'That's right, that's right. And he knows, of course. His parents told him, and other people may have told him. I think he blames me for it. And you know why. But he's the only person in the world who blames me. I'm his own grandmother! People have told me that he wants to get married. *He* has never told me. She's a nice girl, a cousin of the Winloves. But he won't ask her because he's afraid. He thinks he's under some kind of spell or curse. And he's afraid that he'll pass it on to his children. It's all very stupid. But you can help, Leo, if you will.'

'I?'

'Yes, you. You know the facts. You know what *really* happened. And besides me, only *you* know. Edward mustn't believe the foolish stories that he has heard. You know that Ted and I were in love. But it wasn't the ordinary kind of love. It was a very beautiful thing. Do you remember that summer of 1900? It was more beautiful than any summer since. And what was the most beautiful thing in it? It was our love. It was something that anyone might be proud of. Don't you agree, Leo?'

I could not say anything except 'Yes'.

'I'm glad you agree because you made us happy. And we made you happy, didn't we? You were only a little boy, but we trusted you with our great treasure. If we hadn't shown it to you, you might never have known anything about love. But Edward—' She stopped.

'But you can tell him, Leo. Tell him everything, just as it happened. He needn't feel ashamed of it, and he needn't feel ashamed of me. It was a beautiful thing. It wasn't wicked or ugly, was it? And it didn't hurt anyone at all. We had some terrible sorrows, of course. Hugh died, and then Marcus and Denys were killed. Then, in the second war, my son Hugh was killed, and his wife. But she was not a great loss. The sadness wasn't our fault. It was the fault of this wicked

century in which death and hate have driven away life and love. Go to Edward, Leo, and tell him this. You used to love taking our messages, didn't you? And this is another message of love. He has this foolish idea that he can't marry. It hurts me more than anything else. I think every man should get married. You ought to have married, Leo. Why didn't you? But it isn't too late. You might still marry. Don't you feel any need for love? But Edward is young. He's the same age as Ted was in 1900. Tell him he must get rid of his stupid ideas. His grandfather would have had them if I'd let him. Poor Ted, if he had had more brains, he wouldn't have blown them out. You owe this duty to us, Leo. Tell Edward there's no spell or curse except hate in the heart.'

I felt very glad when she stopped. I had tried to stop her several times because she seemed tired. We talked a little more, and then I stood up. I promised to visit her again.

'Bless you!' she said. 'You're the best friend I have. Kiss me, Leo!' Her face was wet with tears.

I went out into the street. Her thoughts and her language were quite strange to me. I was astonished at the way she had deceived herself. She had deceived herself completely for more than fifty years. I could not understand why her words had had a powerful effect on me. And I almost wished that I could deceive myself equally.

I had not promised to give Edward her message of love. I was not a child whom she could order to obey. My car was standing by the post office. It would be easy to telephone Ted's grandson and make an excuse—

But I did not. I drove to Brandham Hall. And on the way I wondered how I would give him the message. Soon I saw the house through the trees.

Exercises in Comprehension and Structure

I. Complete these sentences, using facts from the Prologue and Chapters 1 and 2.

1 Leo and his mother had very few friends because . . .
2 Leo taught Maudsley how to write magic spells in order to . . .
3 Early in May Leo agreed to write a spell in order to . . .
4 Leo would never forget the year 1899 because . . .
5 Mrs Maudsley wrote to Mrs Colston so as to . . .
6 Mrs Colston hesitated and made many excuses because . . .
7 Leo's mother agreed that he would not need summer clothes because . . . (2 reasons)
8 When Mrs Maudsley looked at people it was usually in order to . . .
9 At my first meal at Brandham I sat next to Mrs Maudsley because . . .
10 Leo did not touch the flowers of the deadly nightshade because . . .

II. Put the verbs in brackets into a suitable form. The necessary information is in Chapters 3, 4, and 5.

1 I still believed, partly at least, that I (can) influence the weather: so that night I (prepare) a strong spell which (reduce) the temperature.
2 I wondered who Hugh, or Trimingham, (be); it (be) a nuisance if he (interfere) with Marian's plans.
3 After lunch we (buy) a few more things and (take) the parcels back to the carriage.
4 Later standing outside the cathedral, I (look) up again, and (try) to see the exact place where the high tower (seem) to meet the sky.
5 Mrs Maudsley (rub) the soft material of my suit between her fingers saying she (think) it (be) very nice.
6 If I (want) to bathe I (have to) get my mother's permission, because she (say) that I (be) delicate.
7 On the other side Denys and his friend (float) on their backs; while I (admire) them, Ted Burgess (climb) out of the water.
8 I (feel) quite sure that there (be) some trouble if Marian's wishes (hinder).
9 Marcus said, 'The doctor (come) and he (know) what it is.'
10 Mrs Maudsley (call) me to her and (put) a shilling into my hand, (say) that it (be) for church.

III. Put short words like *on*, *with*, *out*, *down* etc: into the gaps in these sentences. The answers can be found in Chapters 6, 7, 8, 9.

1 I noticed that the name Trimingham appeared — each brass plate — the wall — the church.
2 Doctor Franklin's carriage, — yellow and black wheels, was standing — the front door — the Hall.
3 I remembered what Marian had suggested — me, and putting — my green suit, I prepared to go —
4 I saw in front — me a straw stack — a convenient ladder — it: half of the stack had been cut away, but I could slide — the rest — it.
5 He put the letter — an envelope and stuck it — : I stretched — my hand — the letter.
6 — Lord Trimingham had arrived everyone — Brandham Hall had behaved — a very ordinary way.
7 — first I was annoyed — Marian's suggestion that I should not go — them — these trips.
8 I waited — her smile, but instead she looked — and — the path, seeming annoyed — something.
9 I supposed that the police were looking — Ted Burgess; I remembered looking — the blood — his hands.
10 A mistake made — accident was just as bad as a mistake made — purpose : — so we believed at school.

IV. Put these sentences into indirect speech. They are taken from Chapters 10, 11, 12, 13.

e.g. Ted said, 'I thought perhaps you hadn't got a heart.'
Ted said that he thought perhaps I hadn't got a heart.

1 Ted explained, 'They're not ordinary letters. Marian will miss them, and I'll miss them, too.'
2 'Does Smiler want to have a foal if it makes her ill?' I asked.
3 Denys said, 'We haven't chosen our full team yet.'
4 'Marian knows I can't sing,' he repeated.
5 Ted said, 'I don't know much about cricket. I just hit the ball. Bill Burdock's our captain.'
6 'Father will get tired if he runs a lot,' Denys said. 'I shan't let him run.'
7 I went to him and said, 'I'm sorry, Ted. I didn't really mean to catch that ball.'
8 The speeches continued and at last someone said, 'Now let's have a song.'
9 The audience shouted, 'We're waiting for you Ted. We know you can sing.'
10 Someone said, 'Is it "Angels ever bright and fair"? I think I've got the music for that.'

V. Complete these sentences. The facts are in Chapters 14, 15, 16.

1 Although I admired him, at the same time I was jealous of Ted,

who . . .

2 Again I had no patience with the priest. He was telling us all to feel sorry for our wickedness, which . . .

3 'Nothing is ever a lady's fault,', Lord Trimingham had said. I thought about this remark, which . . .

4 For more than a week I had not visited the rubbish heap, which . . .

5 On my way I thought about Marian's kindness to her old nurse, whom . . .

6 At school I had learned how to treat angry words; but it was different with Marian, who . . .

7 I soon arrived at the gates of the farm, where . . .

8 Marian would have told everyone that I was a stupid and ungrateful boy who . . .

9 Marian's success in charge of the table was very different from her mother's whose . . .

10 But I was anxious to interfere between Marian and Ted, whose . . .

VI. Turn these sentences round, as in the example, so that they are in the *passive*.

  e.g. Sometimes the darkness frightened me.
  Sometimes I was frightened by the darkness.

They are taken from Chapters 17, 18, 19, 20

1 The bright black fruit offered me something I did not want.

2 But I was still afraid of the light from her dark eyes when she looked at me.

3 After the meal we did not discuss any plans for the day.

4 The ninth viscount would never know I had saved him from the fate of the fifth.

5 The bicycle is the chief present, and Marian will give it to you at six o'clock.

6 I wondered how I could spend the day.

7 I did not want to be alone, because she was the main cause of my unhappiness.

8 She was sorry, she said, that she had neglected one of her important guests.

9 We had both forgotten that my birthday party was at tea-time on Friday.

VII. They are taken from Chapters 21, 22, 23. Join these pairs of sentences with *so that* or *because* :

1 He had lied to Marian.
  She would not find Ted near the huts at 6 o'clock.

2 Leo hoped the affair would end.
  It was pushing Ted away from the things he loved.

3 Leo had brought a knife to cut the root of the deadly nightshade.
  He would be able to use every part of the plant.
4 A lot of people had gone mad.
  All the hot weather wasn't natural.
5 Leo asked everyone to excuse him.
  He would be able to read his letters.
6 He was afraid to visit the hut where he had killed the plant.
  He would imagine all kinds of things.
7 Leo tried to think only about the events that actually happened.
  He could try not to use his imagination.
8 Mrs Maudsley asked if Leo and Marian were arguing about the
  letter.
  She had seen it on the ground.
9 At Brandham Leo's magic powers had failed.
  The people there were *not* ordinary.
10 Leo had asked Viscount Trimingham to tell Marian he was there.
  He would not surprise her by his visit.